CRITICS HAIL THE LEGAL THRILLERS OF CHRISTINE McGUIRE

Until We Meet Again
"A great legal thriller . . . that allows readers to see [Kathryn] as a mom, a woman, and an attorney. . . . A fascinating and complex tale."

—Barnesandnoble.com

Until the Bough Breaks
"A provocative story examining the ugly twists of domestic violence . . . sharp legal thriller."

—*Publishers Weekly*

Until Death Do Us Part
"A gripping drama. . . . Readers are treated to three-dimensional human beings filled with fears, doubts, and flaws."

—Amazon.com

Until Justice Is Done
"What sets McGuire's novels apart from the pack is the level of realism she brings to the legal aspects of the story."

—*The Sentinel* (Santa Cruz, CA)

Until Proven Guilty
"A tense, nerve-jangling thriller that should satisfy fans of *The Silence of the Lambs*."

—Peter Blauner, bestselling author of *The Intruder* and *Slow Motion Riot*

Books by Christine McGuire

Perfect Victim
Until Proven Guilty
Until Justice Is Done
Until Death Do Us Part
Until the Bough Breaks
Until We Meet Again
Until the Day They Die
Until the Final Verdict

Christine McGuire

Until the Final Verdict

POCKET BOOKS

New York   London   Toronto   Sydney   Singapore

This book is a work of fiction. Names, characters, places and incidents are products of the author's imagination or are used fictitiously. Any resemblance to actual events or locales or persons, living or dead, is entirely coincidental.

An *Original* Publication of POCKET BOOKS

 POCKET BOOKS, a division of Simon & Schuster, Inc.
1230 Avenue of the Americas, New York, NY 10020

ISBN: 0-7434-2229-5

First Pocket Books printing June 2002

10 9 8 7 6 5 4 3 2 1

For information regarding special discounts for bulk purchases, please contact Simon & Schuster Special Sales at 1-800-456-6798 or business@simonandschuster.com

Cover design and illustration by ZuccaDesign

Printed in the U.S.A.

For Nicole, Jimmy and Steven

Our heartfelt gratitude is extended to

our agents, Richard Pine and Sarah Piel
and to the fond memory of Arthur Pine
without whose encouragement and support
no Kathryn Mackay novels would be in print

and to

our editor Suzanne O'Neill

PROLOGUE

DRIVEN BY AN ALASKAN COLD FRONT, *the first winter storm assaulted Santa Rita with thick sheets of horizontal rain. Whipped into a fury by heavy northwest winds, the cold water slashed through the dark and pummeled the County Courthouse.*

Judge Jemima Tucker stared at herself in the bathroom mirror for a few seconds, then fastened her bra, buttoned her blouse, and smoothed her skirt. She switched off the lights, closed the door, and strode quickly down the cold, damp hall. She stopped at her chambers, inserted the key and swung the door open, but before she could flip the light switch, an arm clamped around her throat from behind.

"Do as I tell you, and you won't get hurt, Jemima. When I let go, walk over and sit behind your desk, and don't make a sound. Nod your head if you understand."

When she nodded, his arm relaxed. By the faint glow of the night lights, she picked her way across the carpeted floor and dropped into her leather desk chair. In the dim light, she couldn't make out his facial expression, but there was no way to ignore the gun pointed at the middle of her chest.

He flipped the barrel tip at the green-glass-shaded antique brass lamp. "Turn on the lamp."

When Tucker's eyes adjusted to the light, she exhaled slowly. "You!"

"Yes, it's me. Stand up."

"Go to hell!"

He cocked the pistol. "Don't be stupid. This gun is small, but it'll kill you as dead as a big one, and I know how to use it. Now, stand up and take off your clothes."

Tucker rose slowly and fumbled with the top button of her silk blouse. "I'll be damned if I'll . . ."

"If you'll what, let me fuck you? How will you stop me?"

Tucker slipped off her blouse, then removed her skirt, panties, and bra. Her flawless chocolate skin erupted in goose bumps, nipples contracting into small, hard, charcoal rocks.

"I must admit you look good for a . . ."

"For a black woman—a nigger?"

"That's such an ugly word. I was going to say 'for a woman your age.' But it's true that I prefer my women to have fairer skin."

"You son of a bitch, I'm not your woman."

"That's what you think."

He pointed at her judicial robe that hung on a rack behind her desk. "Put that on, then sit down."

She dropped the robe over her head and sat.

He duct-taped her wrists behind her back, then pushed her down so her buttocks hung over the edge of the seat, taped her chest to the chair, pushed it away from the desk, and knelt in front of her.

"Spread your legs."

When he finished, he taped her mouth, perched on the corner of her desk, pulled out latex gloves, and blew into them, forcing tiny talcum clouds to float into the air. Then he pulled a package from his pants pocket and removed a shiny stainless steel instrument.

Tucker's scream came out a muffled grunt.

He walked around behind her, stood for several moments, then grabbed her hair, yanked her head back, and stared into her terrified eyes.

"Bitch!" Then he slit Jemima Tucker's throat.

CHAPTER

1

"MY GOD!"

Santa Rita County District Attorney Kathryn Mackay and Sheriff Dave Granz stood just outside the door to Judge Jemima Tucker's chambers. Mackay's dark, curly hair was wet and she was dressed in black Gap jeans, a gray FBI Academy sweatshirt, and black Nine West loafers.

Granz' black Harley-Davidson T-shirt flopped over the waist of his faded Levi's. He ran his fingers through his unruly blond hair and shook his head sadly, but didn't comment.

An older Asian man wearing bifocals, polyester trousers, and a Hawaiian print shirt was documenting the crime scene with an ancient tripod-mounted, manual Nikon. He glanced up when he heard Mackay.

"Hello, Charlie," she said.

Sergeant Charles Yamamoto headed up the Crime Scene Investigation unit—CSI to law enforcement insiders. Short and gaunt, he was a criminalist before Mackay went to law school. His expertise was as well known as his stoicism.

"Awful, Ms. Mackay, terrible. A fine lady."

Mackay had never before seen Yamamoto show emotion, but she knew he was fond of Judge Tucker, who, despite her fearsome reputation among lawyers, was revered by experts like Yamamoto for her respectful treatment when they testified.

"I know."

Yamamoto went back to work while his investigators collected evidence. The lights had been turned off while one investigator passed a special ultraviolet light called a Woods Lamp over the surfaces of the crime scene to reveal stains or foreign materials invisible to the naked eye. A young black woman dusted the desk, file cabinets, and other smooth surfaces for fingerprints, while a third sucked up trace particles from the carpet with a battery-powered vacuum. Its contents would be analyzed by criminalists at DOJ, the Department of Justice, who could often identify a killer from microscopic bits of dirt, fibers, or hair.

"Crime scene's pretty clean," Granz commented.

"Whoever did it might not have left anything."

Mackay's eyes returned to Tucker's corpse, whose almost-severed head lolled back over the chair top, attached only by bone and a thick strand of skin. Her torso was upright, her robe hiked up above her waist.

Blood had gushed from severed jugulars, spilled into her lap, overflown onto the floor, and was coagulating in rust-red puddles.

"Who found the body?" Mackay asked.

"A janitor," Granz answered. "Uniforms got here first, secured the scene, and called Jazzbo Miller. He was on call. Miller called me, then Yamamoto."

"What time did County Comm log the call?"

"Ten-thirty."

"What's a janitor doing here at ten-thirty on Saturday morning?"

"He cleans up every evening after the courts close. He was getting supplies out of a closet in the basement when someone grabbed him from behind, hooked an arm around his neck, and slapped a rag over his nose and mouth. Says it smelled like chloroform—he called it 'ether.' Next thing he knows, he wakes up this morning wrapped in duct tape. Took a while to get free of the tape. When he came upstairs to use the phone, he spotted Tucker and called 911."

"Did he get a look at his attacker?"

Granz shook his head. "Doesn't sound like it."

"Any idea how the killer got in?"

"Not yet, but this'd be a hard building to break in to. Either the killer had a key or he came in before the courts closed and hid until everyone went home."

"Robbery gone bad?"

He shook his head. "Doesn't look like anything's been taken. We'll check her calendar, files, appointment book, voice-mail messages, go through her desk."

"How would he know she was working late?"

"You got me, but whoever it was came after Tucker."

"Well, when you catch him, I hope they strap him to the lethal-injection table."

"Just like that?"

She placed her hand on his arm. "No, not 'just like that.' But in my opinion, death's the only appropriate punishment for a killing this gruesome."

They moved aside to make way for two deputy coroners to enter the room, one of whom released the straps on the gurney and unfolded a heavy black plastic body bag, laid the bag out, and unzipped it.

Granz motioned with his thumb. "Let's step out into the hall."

"Have you called Nelson?" Mackay referred to her close friend Doctor Morgan Nelson. Under California law the Sheriff is also Coroner, but since Sheriffs come from law enforcement rather than medical backgrounds, they hire forensic pathologists to perform autopsies.

"He's meeting my deputies at the morgue."

"Keep me posted."

"You be home?"

"I'll be gone most of the day."

Once lovers, when Mackay found out about Granz' affair with a woman named Julia Soto, she ended the relationship. He had repeatedly attempted to revive it but each time they got close, she got scared and backed away. He hoped she was spending the day with her twelve-year-old daughter, Emma, rather than another man, but didn't ask.

"If anything comes up, page me, otherwise call after five o'clock."

"Okay, Babe."

"I—" Tempted to return the use of their old, familiar term of endearment, she reconsidered. "I've got to go."

CHAPTER

2

"YOU PLAYED REALLY WELL, EM. I'm so proud of you."

"Oh, Mom, you always say that after my violin recitals, no matter what. It's your duty." Emma's expression conveyed the continual state of exasperation she and her friends felt with parents.

Kathryn smiled. "True, but I always mean it. What are you going to eat?" Emma had chosen the restaurant for dinner as a reward for her flawless solo. As expected, she picked the current teenagers' hangout, a fast-food place called Carpo's. Actually, Kathryn liked Carpo's food, and she felt invigorated by the atmosphere, which pulsed with a wholesome energy emanating from the hordes of young people.

"Double bacon cheeseburger, large fries, a slice of chocolate cake, and a Diet Coke."

"I was thinking along the lines of a grilled chicken breast and a side of pasta. What's the point to a diet drink if you're going to eat all that stuff?"

"I don't want to get fat."

"You're slender and beautiful. I just want you to stay that way." Kathryn walked to the counter, ordered and paid for their food, and carried the full tray to the table, where Emma was talking on her mom's cell phone. Kathryn motioned to hang up.

As soon as she punched the End button, Emma told Kathryn, "Ashley and I are getting our belly buttons pierced."

"No way, we've already been through this." Kathryn's look told her daughter there would be no negotiating. "Understood, missy?"

"It's my body," Emma protested weakly.

"I know, but . . ."

"Then, can I get my left ear pierced?"

"It's already pierced."

" 'Nother one." Emma tugged at the small gold ring that hung from her left earlobe. "All the girls are doing it."

Kathryn looked around and noted that most girls had one ear pierced in at least two places, and some had several. "I'll think about it."

When they finished eating, Kathryn went to the rest room and Emma pulled the StarTac cell phone out of her mother's handbag.

"Ash—it worked," she said conspiratorially. "She's gonna let me get my ear pierced again."

She giggled, listened for a minute, then told her friend, "Are you kidding, I'd *never* get my belly button pierced, that'd hurt!" She was still talking when her mother returned.

"Please get off the phone and finish eating, Em."

"What's the hurry, Mother?"

"I'd like to get home by five o'clock."

"What for?"

"Dave said he might call."

CHAPTER

3

EMMA RAN TO THE SPARE BEDROOM of their condo as soon as she and Kathryn got home, checked the answering machine, and yelled, "Mom, there are three messages for you, do you want me to write them down?"

Kathryn had filled a teakettle and put it on the stove, then ground some fresh decaf beans and dumped them into a Melitta filter. She set the filter cone on a cup, then walked to the back bedroom and kissed Emma on the cheek.

"No thanks, sweetie, I'll listen to them in a few minutes. Get busy on your homework."

After her coffee was brewed, she slipped off all her clothes, removed her makeup, washed her face with cool water, put on black Nike sweats, sat at her small desk, and punched the Listen button on the answering machine.

"Hi, Babe, uh, it's Dave. I hope you had a great afternoon. I called to let you know Doctor Death—sorry, Nelson's going to autopsy Tucker this evening."

Kathryn frowned at the use of Nelson's unofficial law enforcement nickname and listened to the second message. "Kate, Dave. Bad news. Berroa escaped. Fill you in tonight."

Eduardo Berroa had been a County Health Clinic doctor who raped several of his Hispanic patients. Kathryn dropped rape charges in exchange for his testimony against County Health Officer Dr. Robert Simmons, who murdered ex-District Attorney Harold Benton and tried, but failed, to murder her as well, before fleeing.

After Berroa testified before the Grand Jury, Kathryn arrested him for a botched abortion that killed one of his patients. She convicted him of involuntary manslaughter and he was sentenced to the maximum, four years in state prison at Soledad.

Berroa's testimony led to a murder indictment of Simmons, but with her first reelection looming, Kathryn's ex-Chief Deputy and political foe Neal McCaskill, criticized her for cutting a deal with a sexual predator, accused her of exercising poor judgment, and cited her prior romantic relationship with Simmons as proof.

Eventually, Mackay tracked Simmons to Tamarindo, Costa Rica, where she had him arrested, only to learn later that he had escaped and disappeared again. Mackay couldn't prove it, but she believed he bought his freedom from sympathetic Costa Rican officials, who at Simmons' extradition hearing openly opposed Mackay's intent to seek the death penalty if Simmons was convicted of Harold Benton's murder.

She punched a phone number into her handset and sipped her coffee.

"Granz."

"What time is Doc Nelson going to autopsy Judge Tucker?"

"How soon can you can get there?"

"I need to make sure Ruth's home."

"And that she'll watch Emma while her mom's out gallivanting again."

"Besides you and Doc Nelson, I don't have all that many friends. Watching Doc autopsy one of them is hardly 'gallivanting.'"

"Gallows humor. I'm sorry."

"It's all right, I know how much you hate these things. Who could blame you after—"

"After the Gingerbread Man smashed in my skull, slashed my throat, and left me to die in that alley? And I damn near did?" He paused. "That night changed my view of death forever, Kate. It almost takes more courage than I can muster to watch an autopsy."

"I know, Dave. Maybe I should go to the morgue by myself. You can read the protocol."

"No, it's my job and I need to be there." He paused. "Good thing Ruth lives in your condo complex, saves you a fortune in gas running Em back and forth."

"Don't want to talk about it anymore, right?"

" 'Bout what?"

"I—"

"See you in thirty minutes," he said, and hung up.

"Love you," she whispered.

CHAPTER

4

"Doc Nelson's waiting for you in the Hellhole."
The security guard recognized the District Attorney
and slipped into law enforcement slang for the
morgue in the basement of County General Hospital.
Edward McCaffrey was a retired Santa Rita cop.

He held the door open for Mackay and added,
"Sheriff's already there."

"Thanks, Ed," Mackay answered.

Like most hospitals, County General's entrance
conveyed a serene cheerfulness with pastel colors,
soft abstract artwork, comfortable furniture, and lots
of glass and skylights.

Mackay crossed the lobby, punched the elevator
Down button, and tapped her toes impatiently. When
the door swished open, she drew in a deep breath

and scrunched up her nose. The morgue's environment stood in stark contrast to the lobby, with its rancid odor of antiseptic and death that ventilators couldn't get rid of, deodorizers couldn't cover up, and she never got used to. Worse was the eerie quiet—as if all living sounds, especially hers, were unwelcome interlopers.

At the far end of the spotless tile hallway was a set of heavy double doors through which hearses loaded and the coroner's wagon unloaded. Putrefying bodies or those with infectious diseases went directly to the isolation suite, where a sealed atmosphere prevented the escape of offensive or infectious gases until high-power exhaust fans sucked them up and blew them into an incinerator.

Other bodies stopped first in the adjacent cold-storage vault. There they were preserved until a morgue attendant known as a "diener" cleaned, weighed, measured, and photographed them in the staging room, then placed them on gurneys and rolled them into one of the autopsy suites.

The largest suite contained three slanted stainless steel tables with high rolled edges to contain blood and other fluids. Each was equipped with faucets, sluices, scales, lockers, a set of autopsy tools, and a soundproof booth where the pathologist dictated notes.

The last suite, called the VIP Room, was used to study special cases and had only one table. Bodies that came to this room often belonged to victims of heinous crimes, and Mackay always approached it reverently.

Granz and forensic pathologist Morgan Nelson were leaning against the wall. Nelson wore blood-splattered green surgical scrubs and plastic covers over his green rubber-soled shoes. A fringe of short gingery hair stuck out around his green skull cap. Years before, he designed and oversaw the morgue's construction, then wrote the operating rules. Like its creator, the morgue operated around the clock with consummate professionalism and efficiency.

Mackay spotted the dark, heavy stubble on Nelson's face and the bloodshot eyes behind his wire-rimmed bifocals and knew he hadn't slept recently.

"You look awful," she greeted him.

"You're a real sweet talker, Katie," he retorted. The nickname was his special privilege as her closest friend. "Worked last night and today, but I knew you'd want this done ASAP."

"TOD?"

"Only way to be exact about time of death is to be there when it happens, but the court building's cold, which slowed down the processes we use to establish time of death—algor, livor and rigor mortis. Body temperature at the scene was sixty degrees, same as ambient. Body temp drops two to four degrees an hour in cold air, so it happened before one-thirty this morning."

"Can you narrow it down a bit?"

"Fully developed livor mortis was present," he told them, referring to the fact that gravity pulls blood to the lowest part of a dead body, where it pools into reddish blotches. "But lividity occurs quickly; besides, there wasn't much blood left, she lived until her heart pumped most of it out."

"Jesus," Granz muttered.

"Body was in total rigor, so she died at least twelve hours before the body was found. Rigor hadn't started to resolve, so I'd say it was closer to eighteen hours, considering room temperature."

"Best guess?"

"Between four o'clock yesterday afternoon and midnight."

"Would vitreous potassium testing firm it up any?"

"Maybe."

"Refresh my memory," Granz said.

"I extract about an ounce and a half of vitreous fluid from the eyeball, and the lab runs a potassium test. Could narrow it down a little, but not much."

"You'll do a rape kit?" Mackay asked, referring to an examination that established whether the victim was sexually assaulted.

"Yeah, of course we need to know if she was raped before death."

"Or after."

"True. The vaginal swabs will tell us if there's seminal fluid present in the vaginal tract, but I can tell you now that there were no external indications of forced vaginal intercourse—no contusions or torn tissue."

"So she wasn't raped?"

"I'd say not, but we'll know more after closer examination of the genitalia."

Nelson pulled two paper scrub suits and four shoe covers from a drawer, which Granz and Mackay slipped into, then they followed him into the autopsy suite where a body lay on the surgical table under a sheet. They had both observed hundreds of autopsies over the years, but neither had ever seen a friend's body stretched out on the table. When Nelson pulled the sheet away from Jemima Tucker's ashen gray corpse, they both gasped audibly.

"I've done more than eight thousand autopsies, and I had the same reaction," Nelson confessed. He slipped on a headset, switched on a recorder, and started dictating the external examination.

"The body is that of a mature, well-developed black female in her midforties, five feet two inches, weight approximately one hundred twenty pounds."

He rolled the body from side to side to examine the back of the torso, then lifted each arm and leg to check underlying tissues. He looked into the ears, nose, mouth, and eyes, then visually inspected the other body openings.

"No visible scars or tattoos, no abnormalities. Outer genitalia normal—no obvious trauma."

He rolled the body onto its right side and slid a brick-shaped, black plastic body-block under the back, forcing the chest to protrude and the arms and neck to fall back. Then he pulled a black-handled Buck knife from a leather case, sharpened it on a sheet of extrafine sandpaper, and drew the razor-sharp blade down an eight-by-ten sheet of paper.

The paper sliced cleanly into two pieces, which he tossed in a trash basket. "Better than a scalpel." He looked first at Mackay, then Granz. "Ready?"

He cut deep V-shaped incisions starting at the

shoulders, curving beneath each breast and meeting at the xiphoid process, or bottom, of the sternum. Another deep cut connected the point of the V to the pubic bone, diverting slightly around the navel. The final cut ran from hipbone to hipbone, intersecting the leg of the Y. He laid back the abdominal skin and peeled skin, muscle, and soft tissue off the chest wall, exposing strap muscles on the front of the neck and the rib cage, then pulled the chest flap up over the face.

"The final insult, losing her identity," Mackay said softly. "Damn, I hate that part."

"Me, too," Nelson acknowledged.

They all pulled masks over their mouths and noses before Nelson ran two quick cuts up the outer sides of the rib cage with a Stryker saw. He lifted out the breastplate comprising the sternum and ribs and laid it on the table, then cut the pericardial sac and pulmonary artery, stuck his finger into the artery and, detecting no thromboembolism, removed the heart. He tied strings to the carotid and subclavian arteries and snipped out the larynx and esophagus. Finally, he cut the pelvic ligaments, bladder and rectal tubes and lifted out the organ block. He inspected it briefly.

"Nothing unusual." He glanced at Granz, who averted his eyes. "I'll weigh and examine the internal organs, but preliminary cause of death is massive hemorrhage from the neck wound. I'll let you know if anything else turns up."

He gave a small flip of the head to Mackay. "Why don't you two get out of here."

Granz sighed. "Gladly."

CHAPTER
5

"I'LL HAVE A TALL DECAF," Kathryn Mackay told a skinny young woman with a purple, green, and yellow buzz cut.

"Gimme a venti dark roast, please." Dave Granz studied the pastry display and reconsidered.

"Since when did you start drinking coffee at ten-thirty at night? It'll keep you awake."

"Prob'ly, but drinking decaf's like washing your feet with your socks on—what's the point? Besides, after what we saw thirty minutes ago at the morgue, I won't sleep anyway."

He paid for their coffee over her objections, and motioned to a lone table at the rear. "Let's sit there so we won't be overheard."

The same table Robert Simmons and I shared our first

time together, she thought, then added silently, *What a screw-up.*

"Overheard?" She glanced around the empty Starbucks and picked a table by the front window. "No one comes here after the mall closes. Wonder why they stay open until eleven."

"Dunno." Granz dropped into a chair across from her. "She was black. Think it was a hate crime?"

Mackay sipped her decaf. "No, there were no racial slurs—no swastikas, no white-power symbols, no *n* word scribbled on the walls."

"Racists leave their calling cards out in plain view, for the shock value, hoping some ignorant editor'll plaster the pictures all over the front page of the paper, get some free publicity."

"If it wasn't racial, what was it? Sex?"

Granz contemplated. "No, the crime scene was too sterile for a crime of passion. She was executed."

"I agree." Mackay nodded. "Sexual sadists usually disfigure a woman's distinctively female features—the breasts or vagina, the inside of the thighs, maybe the face. There was none of that. How does her husband check out?"

"Name's Alejandro Sanchez, an ER doc at Española Community Hospital. As soon as we cleared the crime scene this morning, we drove to their home, but he wasn't there. We contacted him at the hospital to notify him of his wife's death."

"What time?"

"About fifteen minutes before noon."

"How'd he take the news?"

"He asked about the details like he was gathering

information to treat a patient in the ER. Afterward, we offered to drive him home, but he said he wanted to finish his shift and could drive himself. Weird reaction under the circumstances, if you ask me."

"ER docs are trained to stay calm in a crisis. He was probably dealing with it on pure instinct."

"Maybe, but I have a feeling about him. Call it a hunch."

"Where did he say he was late yesterday?"

"He started a twenty-four-hour ER shift at noon."

"Did you run him through National Crime Information Center computers?"

"NCIC turned up nothing." He shoved a sheet of paper across the table. "We need to toss their house."

Mackay glanced at the search warrant. "You're the affiant?"

"I can swear to facts that establish probable cause to search as well as any of my detectives, besides it gives me an excuse to see you."

"Run through your PC with me."

"The spouse is always a suspect until eliminated."

"That won't get you in the front door."

"Whoever killed Tucker knew she was working late, and there was no forced entry. Her husband would know when she was working, and he could easily dupe her keys to the court building and her chambers without her knowledge. Nelson says her throat was cut with something very sharp. Could've been a scalpel. Sanchez is a doctor."

"So was Berroa. Maybe he dropped by Tucker's office."

Granz shook his head. "Berroa's in Mexico by now.

No way he'd chance going back to the joint. Besides, the court building was locked—how would he have gotten in?"

"Maybe he learned a trade at Soledad."

"No way. It all points to Sanchez."

"It's pretty thin, but if we lay it out to the right judge, it might fly. What about her family?"

"None locally. Her parents live in Texas. They told Waco cops Sanchez is originally from Mexico."

"Makes it easy for him to flee. That'll help convince a judge."

"Detective Miller's standing by Tucker's home, waiting for the warrant."

Mackay scanned the warrant and supporting affidavit and signed it. "Who're the on-call judges?"

"Jesse Woods and Reginald Keefe."

"Keefe's a civil lawyer, a political hack, his elevator doesn't go all the way to the top floor, and he's ornery as hell to boot. Woods is an ex-prosecutor and damned smart. He'll cut us some slack on close calls."

"I didn't figure it was that close a call. I called Keefe."

"Jesus, Dave, are you a masochist? The only thing Keefe hates worse than cops and prosecutors is being contacted after hours. Why'd you call him?"

"To piss him off." He stood and started to slip on his black leather jacket, still wet from the rain. "Let's go do it."

She grabbed his hand and pulled him back into his chair. "Can we talk for a minute first?"

"Sure, Babe." He studied her solemn expression. "What's wrong?"

"Seeing Jemima Tucker on that stainless steel autopsy table, and remembering our phone conversation before we went to the morgue, I got to thinking—that could easily have been one of us."

"Nice thought. Do we have to discuss this right now?"

"Yes. Life is short, and for the past couple of years mine has felt incomplete. Each day slips away and leaves a void behind that even Emma can't fill—and shouldn't have to try. Someday she'll go away to college and I'll be alone. I don't want that."

He leaned forward, still grasping her hand. "What *do* you want?"

"Another chance at being a family, if you'll—"

"Kate—"

"Let me finish, or I'll never work up the guts to say it again. What ruined our relationship was both our faults, and I've been afraid to get close again. But protecting myself is making both of us miserable, and being dead inside isn't a solution."

She cleared her throat. "Were you serious when you asked me to marry you?"

"I was never more serious about anything in my entire life."

"Then, I'd like to talk about it."

"When?"

"Soon." She laughed. "But not until we get our search warrant. Keefe's liable to lock us both up for ruining his Saturday evening."

CHAPTER
6

REGINALD AND BONNIE KEEFE LIVED in his family's old estate in Beach Flats, once an exclusive address, more recently the domain of drug dealers, thieves, hookers, and illegals hiding from the INS in rundown shacks where the idle rich once weekended.

Motion sensors detected the unmarked Jeep Cherokee as soon as it turned off the street into the chain-link–fenced entrance and ignited a bank of xenon floodlights. Closed-circuit cameras tracked it to a weatherproof, electronic guard station where Granz punched a button on the keypad marked PLEASE ANNOUNCE YOURSELF.

The squawk box answered, "Who's there?"

Bonnie Keefe had a sexy, thick southern accent and

a body that caused car wrecks when she walked down the street—and the way she dressed gave men plenty to gawk at. She was also a fine lawyer whose opponents in land-use cases called her the Georgia Cobra. In built-out Santa Rita County, her clients' goal was to bulldoze sensitive habitats in favor of tract houses or big-box chain stores. Her job was to make sure they got to do it, and she was very good at her job.

"Sheriff Granz and District Attorney Mackay, Mrs. Keefe," he answered into the speaker.

"Come right in."

The heavy, barbed-wire-topped chain-link gate rolled open. Granz eased the Cherokee up the gravel drive, which ended at a low, single-story cottage covered with wood shingles. Over almost a century, add-on bedrooms, bathrooms, and entertaining spaces had created a hodgepodge of incongruent architecture that somehow worked. Heavy, untended native shrubs and redwood trees shaded the cottage, a detached garage, a swimming pool, and two tennis courts, creating a gracious but untamed environment that couldn't be duplicated by the best landscape architect.

Granz punched the doorbell. "I'll bet this place is worth at least five million bucks."

When the door swung open, Bonnie looked like she'd just stepped out of the shower. Her shoulder-length blond hair was plastered to her head and her strikingly perfect face was devoid of makeup. She wore a clingy red silk robe with a plunging neckline.

"Sheriff Granz, District Attorney Mackay, come in,

please." She stepped aside and raised her right arm in a welcome gesture that pulled the top of her robe partly open, exposing a large purple nipple. She pulled it closed with long, manicured fingers. "Would you like something to drink?"

"No, thank you," Mackay answered, "we'll only be a few minutes."

"All right. Reggie is waiting for you right down the hall, in the kitchen." She turned and walked across the living room, the damp robe stuck to her buttocks. "Then, I'll finish drying off."

Judge Keefe sat at an old chrome-trimmed Formica dining table in the kitchen, sipping an Anchor Steam beer. He was dressed in a pair of faded Levi's and an open-necked denim shirt with the sleeves rolled up above the elbows. Mackay grudgingly admitted to herself that he was a good-looking man, in spite of the ugly scowl that distorted his face.

He glanced up, and slammed the bottle down on the table. "What the hell's so important that it couldn't wait until Monday?"

Granz pulled out a chair and sat down. "I need a search warrant."

Keefe motioned Mackay toward an empty chair. "If he's going to make himself at home without an invitation, you might as well too."

"Thanks, Judge."

"Have you reviewed the warrant?" Keefe asked Mackay. "Granz doesn't get his search unless you've passed on it first."

"I've signed off. There's PC to search the house."

Keefe turned his hand over palm up and wiggled his fingers at Granz. "Then stop wasting my time and let me see the damn thing. Whose privacy do you want to violate this time?"

Granz slid the warrant across the table. Keefe grabbed it, glared at Granz briefly, then dropped his gaze to the paper. He read it, looked up, read it again, dropped the paper on the table, then pushed it back toward Granz with the tip of one index finger, like it was on fire. "Is this a joke? It says Jemima Tucker was murdered."

"She was. Didn't you see the news on TV?"

"We went to a concert in San Francisco this afternoon. Didn't get home till a few minutes ago. When did it happen?"

"Sometime late yesterday afternoon. Her body wasn't found until this morning."

Keefe reached for his beer, but his shaking hand knocked the bottle onto the tiled floor. It shattered with a loud bang, splattering everyone's legs with beer.

No one spoke for a few moments, then Keefe scribbled his name on the warrant and handed it back to Granz. "Please keep me informed about the progress of your investigation, Sheriff."

"That's an unusual request, Judge."

Keefe's voice was soft and low. "I'd really appreciate it."

CHAPTER

7

"WHAT WAS THAT ABOUT?" Granz turned on the windshield wipers and pulled the Jeep out of the Keefes' driveway.

Mackay shook her head. "Damned unusual change in attitude. Maybe he figures he's next."

"Can't overlook the possibility. You want to help us toss Tucker's house?"

"No, I should pick Emma up from Ruth's. If I don't take her home, she won't get any sleep, and Sunday's her homework day."

Granz pulled his Jeep into the empty parking lot in front of Starbucks, beside Mackay's Audi. "I'll call you tomorrow morning and let you know what we turn up."

"Okay." She touched his lips with her fingertips, kissed him on the cheek, and opened the door.

"Kate?"

She stopped with her hand on the Jeep's door handle and leaned back inside.

"Yeah?"

"I've been serious every time I've asked you to marry me. I hope you aren't sorry about what you said earlier tonight."

"Frightened, yes. Sorry, definitely not."

CHAPTER

8

"WHAT TIME IS IT?" Mackay answered the phone on the second ring, still half awake.

"It's only eight o'clock, Babe, but I want to fill you in on our search of Tucker's home. Get yourself some coffee and call me back."

"Okay, give me a few minutes." She tossed the covers off, stretched and yawned, swung her legs over the side of the bed, and stood up, straightening the Santa Cruz Harley-Davidson T-shirt that she almost always slept in, a gift from Dave. She tiptoed into Emma's room, tucked the covers around her neck, gave her a peck on the cheek, then carried the phone into the bathroom. When she had brushed her teeth, rinsed her face, and put on a navy DEA sweatshirt, she brewed coffee and sat at the kitchen counter.

"So, how'd it go?" she asked when Granz answered the phone.

"Told you I had a feeling about Sanchez," Granz began. "We seized a box of size-twenty-two Cincinnati Surgical disposable scalpels. Big ones. They come ten to a box, one was missing."

"The murder weapon could have been *any* sharp instrument, and he's a doctor."

"Sure, but why keep a box of scalpels at home?"

"Point taken. What else?"

"We seized some greeting cards—Christmas, birthday, anniversary, that sort of thing. One of them was an I'm Sorry card. It had a handwritten note inside that said, 'Jemima— Please reconsider. I can't lose you. Let's work things out.' "

"Where was it?"

"A dresser drawer in Jemima's bedroom."

"*Jemima's* bedroom?"

"Looks like she and Sanchez didn't share a bedroom."

"I'll be damned. Did Sanchez write the note?"

"Can't tell, it wasn't signed. We found an invoice for a consultation with Margaret Whittier."

Mackay had started to sip her coffee, but stopped and set it on the counter. "Margaret Whittier?"

"Right, Santa Rita's meaner-than-a-junkyard-dog divorce lawyer. Whittier had written on it, 'J— Call me when you decide.—M.' "

"Did you contact Whittier?"

"Her answering service says she's out of town until Monday. I called Sanchez and set up an interview. Can you make it?"

"Where and when?"

"My office in an hour." He paused. "Sorry, Babe, I know it's Sunday morning, but I wanted to talk to him before he had time to put together an alibi."

"No problem, I'll give Ruth a buzz. Is he bringing his attorney?"

"Didn't say."

"He was married to a judge. She'd have warned him to never talk to the cops without an attorney."

"Let's hope he ignores her advice," Granz quipped.

"I'll fix Emma's breakfast before I take her up to Ruth's." She glanced at the clock and dumped her coffee into the sink. "See you in an hour."

CHAPTER

9

Outside, the five-story concrete County Government Center was ugly at best—on drizzly Sunday afternoons, it was downright depressing. The inside was no better. The ceiling of the Sheriff's third-floor office was a maze of HVAC ducts, electrical cables, and pipes, all sprayed with an ineffective, gray asbestos soundproofing that County officials claimed wasn't a health hazard.

Granz sat behind his metal government-issue desk, wearing faded Levi's, a blue Indian Motorcycles T-shirt, and Sperry Top-Siders. He pulled a Panasonic minirecorder from his center drawer and set it on the desk but didn't turn it on, then leaned back in his chair.

Alejandro Sanchez perched uncomfortably on the

edge of an old, forest-green leather chair facing Granz' desk, his pale blue Armani shirt and charcoal slacks heavily wrinkled. Even with his thick, jet-black hair mussed and his cheeks covered with black stubble, he was astonishingly handsome. His sleepy, bloodshot eyes squinted at Granz through stylish wire-framed glasses.

Mackay sat in the other chair, half turned so she could see Granz and Sanchez. "We very much appreciate your coming here this afternoon, Doctor. It will save us all a lot of time and trouble."

Granz inserted a fresh cassette in the recorder, then nodded.

"Do you mind if we record our conversation? I find it much more accurate than taking notes."

Sanchez shook his head. "I don't mind."

"Thank you." Mackay waited for Granz to flip on the recorder, then announced the date, time, and the name of each person present.

"Are you going to read me my rights?" Sanchez asked.

Granz and Mackay didn't want to run the risk that Sanchez would lawyer up, but they knew that no statement would be admissible in court unless he was advised of his Miranda Rights, and waived them, before a custodial interrogation commenced.

"You're not in custody, Doctor," Mackay said. "You are free to stop cooperating and walk out of this interview whenever you wish. Do you understand?"

"Am I a suspect?"

"In the early stages of a homicide investigation, everyone is a suspect, including family members,"

Granz explained. "To avoid adding to their grief, we try to eliminate them as quickly as possible, and focus on more productive leads."

"I see."

"Do you know of anyone who might want to kill your wife?" Granz asked.

"She's sent hundreds of violent criminals to prison. It wouldn't be surprising if someone hated her enough to kill her."

"Is that what you think happened?"

"I thought it was your job to find out."

"That's what we're trying to do, and we're considering the possibility that it might be someone Judge Tucker sent away. Did she ever mention receiving strange phone calls, threats, or that she was afraid of anyone in particular?"

"She rarely discussed her work with me."

"Anyone else who might bear a grudge against either or both of you?"

"Not that I know of."

"Unhappy ex-spouses or lovers?"

"Don't be ridiculous."

Granz sighed. "I realize some of our questions might be difficult, but the sooner we find out all the important facts, the faster we will catch your wife's murderer. Did either of you gamble, use illegal drugs, or have serious debt or financial problems?"

"Definitely not."

"How would you describe your relationship with your wife?"

"What the hell does that mean?"

"Was your marriage happy?"

"We had our problems, but our relationship was secure and we were happy."

Granz leaned back in his chair. "You weren't aware that she had contacted a divorce attorney?"

Sanchez squirmed and crossed one leg over the other. "Well—I suspected. We'd been arguing lately, and the subject came up. But she wouldn't have gone through with it."

"Arguing about what?" Granz persisted.

"Nothing in particular, just the usual things that married couples argue about."

"They were serious enough that you weren't sleeping together."

"All married couples go through these things. Like I said, she'd have gotten over it."

Granz leaned forward, forearms on his desk, and stared at Sanchez. "Where were you Friday evening?"

"Are you going to arrest me?"

Granz ignored the question. "It'd help if you told us where you were Friday evening."

"Working."

"Hospital records say you signed in at noon Friday, and didn't sign out until noon Saturday, after we spoke with you. But you went out for an hour or so at about six P.M."

"I went to dinner."

"Where did you eat?" Granz flipped open his notebook. "The respiratory therapist paged you several times while you were gone, but you never answered the page."

"It's embarrassing." Sanchez averted his eyes and

hesitated. "I didn't actually go to dinner. I was with someone."

"Who?"

Sanchez shook his head. "I can't tell you her name."

"Why not?"

"She's married."

"We'll verify your story with her as discreetly as possible," Mackay assured him.

"If I don't tell you her name, you'll arrest me?"

"It's a possibility."

"Bonnie."

"Excuse me?"

"I was with Bonnie Keefe."

CHAPTER

10

"Start your homework, honey," Kathryn told Emma as soon as they walked into their condo.

"How do you know I didn't already do it?"

"A mother knows," Kathryn answered. "I'll bet you and Ruth watched a movie. Right?"

Emma tried unsuccessfully to suppress a grin. "*Vertical Limit*," she admitted, then hinted, "It was awesome, 'specially with Ruth's big-screen TV and surround sound."

Kathryn laughed. "Dream on. Now start your homework, I'm going to work out."

When Emma disappeared into her room, Kathryn changed into sweats, turned on the treadmill, grabbed the evidence and property reports from the Tucker crime scene, and started walking at a brisk pace. After about fifteen minutes, her telephone beeped.

"I tried to confirm Sanchez' alibi," Granz reported. "It'll have to wait, the Keefes are away till tomorrow."

"That's not surprising. Keefe was pretty upset about Tucker's death."

"I'd say he was more scared than upset, and decided to get the hell out of town."

"Do you think someone might go after another judge?"

"No, I'm pretty sure Tucker was targeted, but to be safe I'll bump up court security first thing tomorrow morning."

"Not a bad idea."

"Well, enjoy the rest of your Sunday off. I'll call you in the morning. I love you."

"Me, too. Talk to you tomorrow."

Kathryn hung up the phone and climbed back aboard the treadmill, but just got up to speed when the phone rang again.

"Mackay?" It was an unfamiliar man's voice.

Kathryn frowned. "Who is this?"

"Check your office e-mail." The line went dead.

She booted up her laptop, and clicked on Outlook Express. When she punched in her password, the county's e-mail system brought up a blank page with an electronic paper clip in the upper left corner. She clicked the attachment icon.

"Damn!"

"What's wrong, Mom?" Emma yelled from her bedroom.

"Nothing, honey, my computer's acting up."

The telephoto picture was grainy and deteriorated from scanned digitization and electronic transmission, but she recognized Robert Simmons, laughing, standing beside a woman in front of a sign that read:

Clínica de Salud La Playa
Un servicio gratis público
de Ciudad Torremolinos
Provincia de Málaga y
Comunidad Autonoma Andalucia

She inspected the photograph for a moment, then pulled a map of Europe out of a drawer, traced the location with her finger, and dialed the phone.

Dave answered the phone after the first ring.

"It's me. Robert Simmons is in Spain," she said without preamble, then described the e-mail.

"Whoever called you sent the e-mail. Did you backtrack the e-mail address?"

"It was sent from a Borders bookstore public Internet access center in Houston, Texas. Untraceable."

"Berroa?"

"Possible—he could've sent it before he sneaked across the border to Monterrey, where his family lives. What's the difference, we know Simmons is in Torremolinos, on the southwestern Atlantic coast."

"He won't be there long if he finds out we've got a fix on him. I'd better book a flight to Spain ASAP."

"I want to go with you."

"I know better than to try to talk you out of it. I'll assign Miller to head up the Tucker investigation—

hell, that's what my Chief of Detectives gets paid for. I assume you want to keep your office involved?"

"I'll ask Jim Fields to assign someone," Mackay volunteered, referring to her Chief of Inspectors.

"Should I make both our flight arrangements or do you want to make your own?" he asked.

"Could you do it? I need to pack and arrange for Emma to stay with Ruth for a couple of days. And I'd like to cook dinner and spend the evening with her."

Kathryn was loading the dinner dishes into the dishwasher when the phone rang.

"I phoned the Spanish National Police. They had me fax Simmons' photo, fingerprint card, and the arrest warrant. They'll contact Torremolinos Municipal Police in Málaga Province to coordinate Simmons' arrest. We fly British Airways from San Francisco at six o'clock tomorrow morning, change planes at London Heathrow for Barcelona. I'll pick you up in the morning and drive you to the airport."

"Thanks, Babe. Sleep tight."

CHAPTER
11

FOR KATHRYN MACKAY, sleeping on a plane was nearly impossible. Dave Granz stayed awake from San Francisco to London, but slept during most of the flight out of Heathrow. She sat in an aisle seat, and he was in the center, his head resting on her shoulder. When the pilot announced the descent into Barcelona, she nudged him reluctantly, enjoying the closeness.

"Dave?"

"Huh?" He rubbed his eyes with his knuckles.

"You asked me to wake you just before we land."

"Yeah," he mumbled. "I've gotta call Torremolinos. We'll catch a shuttle flight from Barcelona to Málaga, the provincial capital, if they've got Simmons in custody."

"If not?"

"We fly back to London."

She slipped out of her seat. "I think I'll go freshen up."

He nodded, yawned again, pulled the GTE in-flight phone from its cradle in the seatback in front of him, then checked his notebook and keyed in a number.

A few seconds after Kathryn returned to her seat, the wheels of the Airbus-320 touched down on the tarmac, the giant plane bounced once, then settled onto its landing gear. When the howl of the air brakes subsided, she glanced at Dave, who was gripping the armrests so hard that his knuckles had turned white.

"I hate takeoffs and landings," he told her.

"I know you do," she said, then prompted, "Well?"

He reached under his seat and pulled out his carry-on bag. "Better get ready, we have a flight to catch in twenty minutes."

"To?"

"Málaga."

CHAPTER
12

"SHERIFF GRANZ?" The man in the Málaga airport terminal was dressed in a black military-style uniform with field jacket and a stark white shirt, but no visible weapon.

Granz shook the proffered hand. "I'm Granz."

"Captain Ésteban Huerta of the National Police—N.P. we are called. Do you have baggage?"

"Just these two carry-ons."

"Are either of you carrying a firearm?"

"No."

"Very well, then, if you will follow me, we shall be on our way."

Huerta led them to a single gray door marked:

Aduana de Diplomático &
Funcionarios Gobiernos
Por favor presenta su formularios de aduana

He punched a button, a buzzer sounded, then the door swung open into a small room furnished only with a single wooden table and two matching straight-backed chairs. No one else was present.

"This is the Customs station used to process diplomatic and government officials," Huerta explained. "National security and Customs are the responsibility of the Guardia Civil, but the N.P. are empowered to exempt foreign law enforcement officers. I cleared you through customs, so you will only need to present your Customs forms for validation at Torremolinos. It is no more than a formality."

Outside, Huerta leaned in the window of a police car and spoke rapidly in Spanish to the driver, a young man in a blue uniform with TORREMOLINOS POLICÍA on each shoulder patch. His name tag said he was Officer Alonso Segundo, and, unlike his N.P. counterpart, Segundo carried a big automatic pistol in a basket-weave holster.

"¡Hola!" Segundo opened the trunk, placed their bags carefully inside, and returned to the driver's seat.

Granz climbed in behind the driver while Huerta held the rear passenger door open for Mackay, then sat in front beside the driver. Once the car merged onto the highway, Huerta turned sideways and leaned over the seat so he could see Granz and Mackay.

"Simmons is being held at the Torremolinos Municipal Police station," he told Granz. "It will take about fifteen minutes to get there."

"You're sure it's Simmons?" Granz asked.

"I faxed his fingerprints to Madrid. Interpol confirmed his identity."

"Has he made a statement?" Mackay asked.

"In Spain, suspects aren't entitled to a lawyer before interrogation, but I assumed you wish to comply with your 'Miranda Rule.' He is being held incommunicado, pending your arrival. I trust that is satisfactory?"

Mackay nodded. "Definitely, thank you."

CHAPTER

13

THE PALACIO DE CONGRESOS rolled past the right side of the car as Captain Huerta gave instructions to Segundo in rapidfire Spanish. Mackay picked up "estación de policía" and "ayuntamiento."

"Did you catch what he said?" Mackay asked Granz.

Huerta turned around and smiled. "Lo siento, Señora—Corporal Segundo doesn't speak English. I told him to take us to the main police station at the town hall, where Simmons is being held."

"You have more than one?" she asked.

"Sí, a substation near Meliá Costa del Sol Hotel, mostly to assist tourists. Incidentally, I reserved you rooms for tonight. The Meliá is convenient to the beach and shopping, if you have time to indulge yourselves."

Segundo stopped in front of El Ayuntamiento, a whitewashed stucco building from whose flat roof the Spanish and Andalusian flags flapped furiously in an onshore breeze. Huerta escorted Granz and Mackay inside the marble-floored foyer, where an archway opened to the police station. A receptionist buzzed them past a security door into a tile-floored corridor.

Huerta stopped at the first door on the left and held it open. It looked like every detective's room in every police station in the world: institutional gray walls, several metal tables, and half a dozen beat-up chairs. One table held a steaming coffeepot and half a dozen cups, one filled with cigarette butts.

He pointed at the wall. "Simmons is waiting for you in the interrogation room on the other side of that one-way mirror."

Simmons sat in a metal chair, an empty coffee cup on the table in front of him, wearing a dark blue jail jumpsuit. His head snapped up at the sound of the door opening. He frowned when he realized Granz was with her.

"I figured you'd come personally, Kathryn. Did you have to bring *him?*"

Granz and Mackay sat in chairs across the table. "Give us any attitude, we'll let Captain Huerta transport you to their prison in Málaga," Granz told him. "It's not a nice place, and you won't buy your way out this time."

"I'm afraid you're right, I tried as soon as they arrested me. Cops in Spain are paid better than in Costa Rica, and more ethical."

"Then you have a problem," Mackay told him. "Do you want to talk?"

"I'm entitled to an attorney before you interrogate me."

Granz shook his head. "You can't tell us anything we don't already know. We came to take you back to stand trial, not to interrogate you."

"Then why talk to me at all?"

Granz leaned forward, elbows and forearms on the table, and stared at Simmons. "It'll take months to process an extradition order through the courts in Madrid. Until that happens, the N.P. will hold you at the provincial prison in Málaga, where a rich, smart-ass gringo's life isn't worth a hundred pesetas. By the time the extradition order goes through, we'll be hauling your body back to Santa Rita in a plastic bag."

Simmons looked at Mackay. "So, what's the point of this discussion?"

Mackay took a sheet of paper out of her briefcase and slid it across the table.

Simmons read it and looked up.

She explained. "Under the U.S.-Spain Extradition Treaty, you sign this extradition waiver, the local court certifies it, we fax it to the Spanish Ministerio de Justicia and the U.S. Embassy in Madrid. We'll be on our way home in twenty-four hours."

"Home! That's a laugh." Simmons thought for several seconds and ran his fingers through his hair. "You'll have the N.P. hold me here rather than Málaga?"

Granz nodded. "We don't want to stay any longer than necessary."

"May I use your pen?" Simmons asked.

Mackay handed him her black Mont Blanc roller ball, a birthday gift from Granz several years before. Granz grabbed it and handed it back to her, then gave Simmons a beat-up PaperMate.

Simmons picked the pen up, studied it, started to sign, then replaced it gently on the table. "There's one thing," he said.

Granz grabbed the PaperMate. "Give him a break and what does he give us back? Bullshit. Let's book a flight to Madrid and let N.P. send him to Málaga."

"No!" Simmons' voice rose. "Hear me out."

"Make it fast," Granz told him.

Simmons looked at Mackay. "When you tried to extradite me from Costa Rica, you insisted on seeking the death penalty."

Mackay's eyes narrowed. "You commit a capital crime, you face the maximum penalty."

"Why should I waive extradition if I'm looking at the death penalty? I'll take my chances at Málaga, maybe I'll find a money-hungry guard. At least I won't rot on death row waiting for the State to kill me. I can die here without knowing when it'll happen."

Mackay lifted her shoulders. "*Your* funeral."

Simmons ignored the pun. "Here's my offer—I'll waive extradition right now if you agree in writing to not seek the death penalty."

Mackay grabbed the paper. "Forget it."

Granz stood and tapped her on the shoulder. "Can we talk outside?"

In the hall, he said, "You'll never get a death sentence in Santa Rita, Babe."

"I'll force a change of venue."

"Prosecutor can't file for a change of venue."

"I said I'd *force* one, not *file* one. I'll make pretrial publicity so ugly he can't get a fair trial in Santa Rita."

Granz stared at her. "In all the years we've known each other, I've never heard you threaten to do anything unethical."

"What's unethical is letting a monster like Simmons off with less than he deserves. And he deserves to die."

"You can't be judge, jury, and executioner."

"Yes I can."

"Take his deal, Kate."

"All right, but I'll never forget you saved that bastard from dying."

CHAPTER

14

Huerta and Granz chatted in the front seat of the unmarked police car as it crept down the narrow streets from El Ayuntamiento. Mackay gazed silently out the rear-seat window at the tightly packed houses with red tile roofs, but as they approached La Zona Playa, homes yielded to tidy iglesias, mercados barrios, restaurantes, and other commercial structures, all built in the same clean Mediterranean style.

The Beach Zone's main street, Paseo Marítimo, was bordered on the ocean side by Playa del Bojondillo; to landward, standing shoulder to shoulder, were highrise hotels that sprouted from the beach and hillsides like whitewashed stucco weeds.

Huerta pulled into the Meliá Costa del Sol Hotel valet station, switched off the engine, flashed a badge at the doorman, and held the door open for Mackay.

Granz grabbed their bags and handed them to a bellman, who hovered discreetly.

"We should receive the court order for Simmons' extradition by noon tomorrow," Huerta told them.

"Should we make flight reservations?"

"I'll do it. Spanish law grants N.P. authority to bump other passengers off any airline, if necessary."

"Gracias."

"De nada." Huerta pointed to the southwest. "If you prefer to not eat at your hotel, La Carihuela—the original fishing village—is a few blocks that way. Along the Paseo are many good marisquerías— seafood restaurants." He checked his watch. "One of my officers will pick you up at nine A.M. tomorrow."

They entered the huge, marble-floored, open-air lobby and Kathryn excused herself to use the ladies' room. She returned to find Dave watching TV on a lobby sofa, two frosty bottles of beer on the glass-topped table. When he spotted her, he turned off the television.

"The rooms aren't ready yet," he told her.

She sat down beside him, leaned back to rest her head on the sofa back, closed her eyes, and hugged her arms to her chest.

He studied her for a few seconds, then leaned forward and picked up his beer, which left a wet ring behind. He sipped the beer, wiped the table, and set the bottle back on the damp napkin. "You haven't said a word for the past hour. What's wrong?"

She opened her eyes. "I screwed up by giving up the death penalty so Simmons would waive extradition. I should have let him stew in the Málaga prison while I petitioned the Spanish Supreme Court."

"He wouldn't have lived long enough for you to get the order."

"No big loss."

"The court could deny your petition."

"They could, but I'd push the State Department to apply pressure. Under our treaty with Spain, they'd order him extradited eventually."

"Could've taken months, maybe years."

"Justice isn't always expedient."

He slipped his arm around her shoulder. "Your sense of duty and justice sometimes makes you impractical, Babe. The deal made sense because no Santa Rita jury would sentence him to the death penalty."

She sat up. "The penalty should fit the crime, and if a criminal ever deserved the death penalty, Simmons does. If a jury's too wimpy to give him what he deserves, at least I'd know I did my job."

"You always do your job."

"I do my job best by being a strong advocate! I'm not sure I should've listened to you."

Dave sighed. "I'll take responsibility if it makes you feel better."

"It doesn't." She paused. "Oh, damn, I apologize. You didn't talk me into anything, I made my own decision. It's just that in retrospect I think it was the wrong one."

"Maybe, but you can't second-guess yourself." He checked his bottle and found it empty. "Aren't you going to drink your beer?" he asked.

"I'm not thirsty." She surveyed the lobby. "Nice hotel."

"Don't want to talk about it anymore, right?"

"Right."

He picked up the TV remote, punched the On button, and scrolled through the channels until he found something he liked.

"How can you watch so much football?"

"This is Europe, Babe. It's soccer."

"Same thing. Why don't you check on our room."

"Huerta booked two adjacent rooms."

"Cancel one of them."

CHAPTER

15

SHE HAD NAPPED for half an hour when Granz sat on the edge of the bed. She was sleeping on her stomach, and he started massaging her back.

She yawned, but made no attempt to roll over. "I must've fallen asleep."

"You did."

He kneaded deeply along both sides of her spine, and she moaned contentedly.

"Jazzbo Miller called a few minutes ago," he told her. "Bonnie Keefe denies being with Sanchez the night Tucker was murdered."

"Really? I believed him."

"Me, too."

"Did they follow up with Sanchez?"

"Not yet."

"Well, we can't do anything about it from here. Besides, I don't want to talk about work anymore."

"Me, neither."

He continued to massage her for several minutes. "Wanta get something to eat?"

"Not yet."

She rolled over, letting his hand slip inside her robe, then she untied it and pulled it open.

He caressed her breast. "I love you."

His other hand started at her ankle, moved up to her calf, the back of her knee, then her thigh. Slowly, he massaged both inner thighs in gradually expanding circles, each pass of his fingertips brushing against her pubis with increasing intensity.

She gasped when his fingers found her warm, soft wetness and slipped inside. Her hand squeezed the front of his Levi's. His fingers probed, teased, tantalized. She responded, but then grasped his hand to stop its movement and prolong the moment.

"I want you in me," she whispered. "I want to make love with my future husband."

CHAPTER

16

By the time they walked to the Paseo de la Carihuela, the deepening purple evening sky had melted into the water at the horizon. Tourists and shoppers crowded the walkway that separated the sand from the cafés and shops, and umbrellas still dotted the beach.

The outdoor courtyard-garden of La Comida de los Pescadores adjoined the esplanade, but well-placed potted plants shielded their table from the view of passersby. They held hands and sipped Spanish Chablis while they waited for dinner. They ate slowly, and when the waiter cleared the table, Dave asked Kathryn if she wanted dessert.

"No, I want to go to that Catholic church we passed walking here."

"What for?"

"To speak with the priest."

"About what?"

"A favor I want him to do for us tomorrow morning."

"I don't get it. What favor?"

"You'll see."

CHAPTER
17

"¡Buenos días! I apologize that my officer didn't pick you up this morning until almost ten-thirty. Was your evening at the Meliá satisfactory?"

Granz and Mackay sat in high-backed chairs facing Captain Huerta's desk.

"Yes, but this morning was even better," Granz told him.

"Did you walk to La Carihuela for breakfast?"

"We went to church."

"Many people visit our ancient church to admire its beauty. Did you enjoy it?"

"We sure did." Granz glanced at Mackay, who nodded permission. "We were married there this morning."

"Married! Congratulations!"

"Gracias."

Huerta handed Granz an official National Police envelope. "After your news, this seems rather ordinary, but the Tribunal Supremo—the Supreme Court—faxed Simmons' extradition order from Madrid about fifteen minutes ago."

Granz opened it and pulled out a stack of papers.

"Three sets of travel documents," Huerta explained, "exit visas, departure-tax exemptions, airline tickets and boarding passes—seats 6A, B, and C on each flight. I assumed you prefer to sit in the forward section of the plane, with your prisoner between you."

Granz passed the envelope to Mackay. "Excellent."

"From Málaga to Barcelona you fly on Air Europa Líneas Aéreas, then British Airways from Barcelona to London, and London to San Francisco. You arrive at four twenty-five this afternoon, California time."

Huerta stood and extended his hand to Granz, then to Mackay. "If you will wait here while I place Simmons in restraints, one of my officers will drive you to the airport, help you clear Customs, and secure the prisoner on board the plane. Shortly before takeoff, he will release Simmons to you, and ask you to sign a custody receipt."

He walked to the door, opened it, then turned. "It has been my pleasure to work with you. You have a long, tiring flight ahead of you. Vaya con Dios. And again, my congratulations on your marriage."

CHAPTER
18

"WHAT TH' FUCK YOU MEAN I can't have another beer? I paid for my ticket." The man's voice was loud and deep, his words slurred. In the aft cabin, two flight-crew members talked to the unruly passenger.

The elderly woman across the aisle from Granz leaned over and wiggled her finger. *"Psst."*

Granz leaned into the aisle toward her and caught a whiff of alcohol on her breath. "Yes, ma'am?"

"My name's Priscilla." She pointed at Simmons. "What'd he do?"

"I'm not at liberty to say, Priscilla."

She nodded conspiratorially. "Official police business. I understand."

"I told you to get me a beer!"

"My husband Nigel always drank too much

when he flew, too, God rest his soul," Priscilla whispered. "Maybe they shouldn't serve liquor on airplanes."

"No, ma'am."

She opened her purse enough to show him her tiny flask. "I always carry my own."

"Yes, ma'am." Granz sat back up.

The flight attendant's name tag said ANDREA. She waited for Granz and Priscilla's conversation to end, then pushed her cart past them, stopped it between seats 8C and 8D, and locked the wheels. "What would you like to drink?" she asked Mackay.

"Diet Coke, please."

A loud crash from the aft cabin was followed by a stream of obscenities.

Andrea checked her watch, then scooped ice into the plastic cup and filled it with Diet Coke. "Less than an hour to San Francisco. He started acting up about an hour ago when the steward told him he'd had enough alcohol." She handed the cup to Granz. "Lately it seems we don't make a transatlantic flight without at least one obnoxious drunk."

Granz passed the drink to Mackay, lowered the tray on the back of the middle seat for Simmons, then did the same for himself.

"I don't want nothin' to eat, I want a beer."

Simmons smiled at the stewardess. "I don't think I want a Diet Coke, Andrea. I'll have whatever that guy's drinking." He tried to point toward the commotion with his right hand, but the handcuff attached to the armrest kept it from moving more than a few inches.

"We'll stick with Diet Cokes," Granz told her.

"I'll get my own beer!"

Andrea poured two more cups of Diet Coke. Before she could hand one to Simmons, a huge, shaggy-haired man with a bushy black beard, florid cheeks, and a huge beer belly hanging out of his black T-shirt charged up the aisle. He staggered around the cart, grabbed a handful of plastic straws and two cans of Coors, popped a tab, and downed half a beer in a single gulp, then spilled the rest on Priscilla. He handed her a wad of napkins. " 'Scuse me."

Andrea set the cups on the cart and reached for the drunk's beer, but he pushed her away. Granz stood up, grabbed at the drunk, but missed.

The drunk flipped Granz the finger. "Mind yer own bizness, asshole." Then he ran up the aisle, smashed into the partition between coach and first class, stumbled into the forward lavatory, and locked the door.

Granz ran forward and pressed his ear against the lavatory wall. He heard a beer-can tab snap open, and banged on the door.

No answer.

He knocked again.

"Get . . ." He heard the man burp, retch, and throw, then the toilet flush. "Get lost."

Granz heard a beer can fall to the deck and waited several minutes, then rapped on the door again.

No answer.

Andrea peered cautiously over Granz' shoulder. He raised his voice. "Police! Open the door."

No answer.

Andrea tapped Granz on the shoulder. "Officer?" She was holding the service phone. "Should I call the cockpit?"

"Not yet. Let's see if I can handle this without any further trouble. Can you check the manifest and tell me the man's name?"

"I did, as soon as he started acting up. Jeremiah Randall."

Granz nodded and knocked on the door. "Mr. Randall?"

No answer.

Granz heard a crash. He knocked again, harder. "Randall, open the door so we can talk."

No answer.

"You can open this door from the outside, right?"

Andrea handed him a key. Granz inserted it slowly and silently, listened, then twisted. When the lock snicked open, he cracked the door and looked inside, then motioned for the flight attendant. "Give me a hand, please, Andrea."

Randall had passed out, wedged in the corner of the tiny room, his head resting on the commode. Vomit stained the front of his T-shirt and dripped from his beard, and a smelly stain spread from the crotch of his Levi's. Two empty beer cans rolled around on the deck between his legs.

Granz, Andrea, and a steward dragged him to an empty row in first class, laid him across the seats, and snugged the seat belt over his waist.

Granz handcuffed him to the armrest and returned to the bathroom, picked up the empty beer cans and dumped them in the trash. "I'll be damned," he muttered. He locked the door and told Andrea, "Don't let anyone use the lavatory."

"Kathryn, can you come with me for a minute?" Granz called out. "And bring your camera."

She pulled her tiny Elph from her purse. When she stepped over Simmons, he reached up with his unshackled left hand and touched her crotch.

"Keep your hands to yourself."

"You used to like it."

In the lavatory, Granz showed her a neat line of white powder about a quarter-inch wide by an inch long and a razor blade on the vanity.

"Cocaine," Mackay said. "He was snorting."

"Looks like he passed out before he could snort the other line. Shoot a few photos before I secure this as a crime scene."

"Done."

When she finished, he swung the lavatory door closed. "I'll have the flight crew radio ahead to arrange for FAA investigators to meet the plane in San Francisco."

"Okay. If you've got things under control, I'd better get back and keep my eye on Simmons. Who knows what he's up to."

When she returned, she sat in Granz' aisle seat. Simmons was chewing on a piece of ice from an empty cup. She leaned her head back and closed her eyes.

He reached out for the cup, picked it up, then suddenly dropped it. He collapsed against Mackay, his eyes widened, his face blanched. Then he groaned. Frothy saliva ran from the corners of his mouth. "My . . . pain . . . chest."

He grabbed his shirt collar, convulsed, then released a deep breath, convulsed again, stiffened, fell face forward against the seat in front of him, and lay still.

Kathryn reached up and punched the flight attendant Call button, groped in her purse, pulled out a small cylindrical key, and unlocked the handcuffs.

Granz heard the commotion and raced back. "He's having a heart attack," she told him. "Help me get him on the floor."

They slid him into the aisle and rolled him onto his back. Granz looked up. "Andrea, find a first-aid kit and get an airway. Fast!"

He pressed his fingers against Simmons' throat. "No heartbeat."

Andrea returned and handed him a flat, curved, clear plastic tube. He inserted it into Simmons' throat and told Mackay, "Start heart compressions while I resuscitate him." Then he told Andrea, "Find out if there's a doctor or paramedic on board."

Minutes later, Andrea leaned over his shoulder. "I'm sorry," she told them. "Flight attendants asked every passenger, and I checked the passenger list. There's no medical personnel on the plane."

Simmons' lifeless face was white, his eyes open, vacant, and glazed. Granz removed the airway and put his hand on Mackay's arm. "It's no use, he's dead."

"Damn!"

"Help me put him in a seat."

When Simmons' body was secured in the first-class section across the aisle from Randall, Granz led

Mackay to the passageway behind the cockpit and hugged her.

"You okay?"

"Not really."

"You did everything possible."

"I guess."

"I'll ask the flight crew to radio ahead and have the San Francisco Coroner stand by."

She pulled back and shook her head. "I want Nelson to do the autopsy."

"He had a heart attack. Let San Francisco autopsy him and send Nelson the protocol."

"He was our prisoner."

"The San Francisco Coroner's gonna be pissed."

"Just be one less autopsy they have to do." She checked her watch. "It's only four P.M., the courts are still open. If you think they'll be a problem, I can get a court order before we land."

He thought it over. "No need. I'll call my deputy coroner and arrange for him to pick up the body at baggage."

"Thanks."

"It's going to take a while in San Francisco to make all our reports."

She glanced at Simmons' corpse. "What's the hurry? He isn't going anyplace."

CHAPTER

19

"SHIT." Lieutenant James "Jazzbo" Miller dragged deep on his filtered Camel and picked up his desk phone. "Miller."

"This is Deputy Rafael Cruz, Judge Tucker's bailiff. I need to talk to you."

Miller ran his fingers through his thick red hair and blew a smoke ring at the No Smoking sign on his office wall, a relic from his boss Dave Granz' tenure as Sheriff's Chief of Detectives.

"What's on your mind, Cruz?"

"I'd rather not talk over the phone. I'm down in the Tombs." It was an apt nickname for the impregnable bunker beneath the court building, where inmates were held, often for hours, while waiting for their cases to be called on the floor above.

Miller sucked in another lungful of smoke and checked his watch. "It's almost five o'clock. I was just on my way out. Can't it wait till tomorrow?"

"I don't think it should."

"Be there in fifteen minutes."

Jazzbo Miller was overweight, with a ruddy complexion, a full beard, and a tobacco-yellow smile. The nickname derived from his avocation as a trombonist in a jazz combo.

He punched his ID number into the electronic security panel and swung the door open. Except for a bench around the perimeter, poured as an integral part of the concrete wall's construction, the vast room was devoid of furnishings or conveniences. Steel rings set into the walls above the bench were used to shackle waiting in-custodies, and two wooden doors accessed tiny cells where violent inmates or those who posed special security risks were segregated. The floor sloped to the middle, and iron grates were bolted over drains every ten feet down the center of the room. A door at the far end, identical to the one through which he had entered, accessed a subterranean tunnel between the Tombs and both the jail and the women's detention facility across the street.

Rafael Cruz was twenty-six, short, stocky, and looked like he spent all his spare time at World Gym. Even with less than two years on the job, he projected an air of quiet competence. "I think Tucker was having an affair."

"You *think?* Just tell me what you know, I'll sort it out."

Suddenly, a heavy-duty electrical relay kicked in,

an electric motor whined, bogged down under load, then a loud sucking noise was followed by the sound of rushing water.

"What's that?" Miller asked.

"Sump pump," Cruz explained. "When they excavated the Tombs, the floor was below groundwater level. Water seeps in and the pump dumps it back into the river through a series of pipes."

He thought for a moment. "A few months back, Tucker's husband was calling two or three times a day and if court was in session, she'd call a recess to talk to him. A couple of times I knocked on her door and heard her crying. She seemed upset—you know, like someone having marital problems."

"That made you think she was having an affair?"

Cruz shook his head. "A couple of months ago, the calls stopped. About the same time, I noticed Keefe spending a lot of time in Tucker's chambers."

"Reginald Keefe?"

"Yeah."

"It's not unusual for judges to meet in chambers to discuss a case. How long did their visits last?"

"Long enough, if you catch my drift. And they spent their coffee breaks together almost every day, sometimes in the cafeteria, usually in her chambers. Lunch hours, too."

"Anything else?"

"The day before she was killed—last Thursday—I went for a run at noon, along the trail by the river. I was just approaching the base of the footbridge that crosses over to the theater when I spot Keefe and Tucker about halfway across, walking close together.

I guess they couldn't see me because of the trees. Anyway, Keefe looks around, probably to be sure nobody's watching, then puts his hand on Tucker's shoulder. She slips her arm around his waist and he leans over and kisses her. Just a quick peck on the lips, but then he looks around, kisses her again, then they keep walking like nothing happened."

"You sure about this?"

"I know what I saw. Tucker and Keefe were having an affair."

CHAPTER

20

BEFORE STEPPING OUT of the elevator, Granz took several deep breaths, sucked the last one deep into his lungs, and held it while he hurried down the hall past the empty gurneys and swung open the office door.

Morgan Nelson removed his reading glasses, stood up, and held out his hand. "Congratulations, Dave. Katie called me last night."

Granz shook the water off his raincoat and draped it over a stack of banker's boxes filled with old autopsy protocols. "I got lucky."

Nelson sat back down and motioned Granz to do the same. "You both did."

Granz studied Nelson's face, which was even more solemn than usual. "You don't seem that happy, Doc."

"Just tired."

Not much bigger than a walk-in closet, Nelson's office contained only a desk and chair, an old wooden visitor's chair, and a metal bookcase full of dog-eared medical references. Floor-to-ceiling shelves overflowed with diplomas, awards, newspaper clippings, forensic journals, medical paraphernalia, and specimen jars containing human brains and tissue samples preserved in formaldehyde.

"Sorry to ask you to come so early," Nelson said.

"No problem. When you called at eight, I'd been at my office for over an hour, catching up on the paperwork that didn't get done while we were in Spain. Besides, it sounded important."

"It is. Tucker's rape-kit results came back positive for semen on one of the vaginal swabs."

"So, she *was* raped."

Nelson shook his head. "There were no vaginal tears, lacerations, or abrasions."

"She had consensual sex before she was killed?"

"Looks like."

"How long before?"

"DNA tests can't tell us how old a biological sample is or when it was deposited, but sperm in the semen migrate up the ovarian tract or degrade quickly. If we recover sperm from the vagina, it's usually not more than twenty-four to forty-eight hours old—seventy-two hours at most."

Nelson rubbed his bloodshot eyes, then ran a hand over the stubble on his chin, clasped his hands on his desk, and leaned forward.

"There's more. One of the anal swabs came back positive for semen, as well."

"From the same sexual encounter?"

"Impossible to tell. There were no tears or abrasions but the swabs also revealed traces of a lubricant, so it was probably consensual anal sex. Until the DNA test results come back, we won't know if both deposits were left by the same man, two men, or several men. Even then it won't be much help unless you have someone to compare."

Granz crossed his right leg over his left, then quickly brought Nelson up to speed on the suspicions Deputy Cruz had related to Miller.

"She had sex before she was killed," Granz summed up, "probably with Keefe or Sanchez. I'll get a search warrant to seize their blood standards for comparison."

"That won't tell you whether the man—or men—who deposited the semen murdered her. It's possible she had sex with Keefe *and* Sanchez within forty-eight hours of her death, but neither killed her."

"True. How long before the DNA results come back?"

"Could be twenty-four hours or a couple of months. Depends on whether or not the lab puts it on the back burner."

"Call Building Forty-six-A, hustle 'em up," he told him, using cop jargon for the Department of Justice lab at 46A Research Drive.

"I'll try."

Granz started to stand, but Nelson motioned him

to sit. "One more thing. I autopsied Simmons last night."

"And?"

"No atherosclerosis."

"Give it to me in language I understand."

"No accumulation of plaque deposits in the lining of the arteries—no evidence of coronary heart disease, disorders of the heart valves, or diseases of the heart muscle or pericardium."

"Doesn't make sense."

"Judging from what Katie told me, I agree. Tell me exactly what happened on that plane."

When Granz finished, he asked, "When you chased the drunk into the lavatory, where was Kate?"

"With Simmons."

"The whole time?"

"Except when I had her bring a camera to take photographs. She went back to her seat while I secured the crime scene."

"Then what?"

"She yelled for me to help resuscitate Simmons."

"How long after Kate went back to her seat did Simmons collapse?"

"A few minutes."

"Had Simmons been eating or drinking anything?"

"The flight attendant poured him a Diet Coke, but he never got it because the drunk crashed into her cart. What's up with all these questions?"

"Just trying to figure out what happened."

"Simmons had a heart attack."

"No, it wasn't a myocardial infarction."

"If it wasn't a heart attack, what killed him?"

"I won't know for sure until I get the blood-toxicology report. But when I do, the question might not be *what* killed him." Nelson cleared his throat. "Have you and Katie moved in together?"

"Not until after we tell Emma this weekend. Why?"

"I might need to talk to you before next week."

CHAPTER

21

Dave Granz opened one eye and squinted at the clock on the nightstand. "Hello."

"Dave, Morgan Nelson. I'm glad I caught you at home instead of at Kate's."

"We're going to tell Emma today, then we'll figure out where to live. What's up at seven o'clock on Saturday morning?"

"We need to talk."

"Sure, when?"

"Fifteen minutes?"

"I can't get to my office that fast, make it an hour."

"How about I come to your house, then?"

"I'll have coffee waiting."

He slipped on a pair of faded Levi's and Fila thongs, then rummaged through a dresser and pulled out a Harley-Davidson T-shirt with a bald eagle gripping lightning bolts in both talons. The front showed a biker with one leg over a candy-apple-red ElectraGlide. Arched over the biker's head, the logo said, RELEASE YOUR LIGHTNING, FEEL THE THUNDER.

He slipped the worn shirt over his head, filled a water pot and set it on a burner, ground fresh Sumatran beans and dumped them into paper filters, then placed the cones over two clear-glass mugs that he had preheated with hot tap water.

After he brushed his teeth and made his bed, he tossed the remains of Friday night's dinner with Kathryn—four almost-empty Chinese take-out cartons, three empty Corona Light beer bottles, and an empty pint of Baskin-Robbins chocolate chip ice-cream—into the garbage.

The doorbell rang just as he finished pouring boiling water over the coffee grounds. When he opened the door, he found Nelson wearing a sweatshirt over wrinkled green surgical scrubs.

"You're a damn workaholic. Do you ever sleep?"

"When it's unavoidable. Can I come in?"

Granz led him to the kitchen and handed him a steaming cup of coffee, then pointed at the leather sofa. "Let's sit in the living room.

"I'm not complaining, but I can't recall the last time you came to my home. We'll do better when it's Kate, Emma, and me living together."

"The last time was when I brought you home from Quick Doc Box after that fiasco with Julia Soto."

Granz closed his eyes and reopened them slowly. "The morning after she accused me of raping her, and they threatened to throw my ass in the slammer if I refused a suspect kit so they could gather evidence to hang me. Not one of my best days."

"Mine, either, but I knew you didn't rape her."

"What if Kate hadn't *proven* I didn't?"

"Wouldn't have mattered."

"Besides Kate, you were the *only* person who believed me."

"I know you."

He studied his friend, who sipped silently at his coffee.

Nelson stroked his chin with his fingers, started to say something, but stopped.

"Something's on your mind, Doc—spit it out."

"You and Katie being married makes it harder."

"What does that mean?"

"I don't know how to say it, so why don't I let this do the talking for me." Nelson slid a folded sheet of paper out from under his sweatshirt, hesitated, then held it out wordlessly.

Granz read it quickly, looked up, and reread it carefully. "This says Simmons died of a drug overdose."

"Digitalis, to be exact."

"Simmons murdered Hal Benton with digitalis to make it look like a routine heart attack."

"And it did, if any heart attack can be called 'routine.' Digitalis is one of the most potent heart medications ever developed, and one of the most lethal. It's a fine line between a therapeutic dose that restores a heart to normal functions, and a fatal dose that induces palpitations, arrhythmia, and tachycardia, then total cardiac arrest and death within minutes."

"Heart attack symptoms."

"Yes, symptoms a physician might misdiagnose, like I did with Benton—if someone he trusted intentionally misled him."

"Someone like Simmons."

"Simmons was a damn fine physician. When he said Benton died of a heart attack, like a fool I didn't question it."

"You had no reason to question it."

"Like hell! I didn't even run a tox screen on Benton's blood until I suspected that Simmons—someone I trusted—was lying to conceal his crime."

"Why would you have thought he was concealing something?"

"Because it's my job to suspect everything and everybody. I didn't make the same mistake this time."

"We searched Simmons before he boarded the plane. He had no drugs on him, much less a stash of digitalis."

"That's my point, Dave. He didn't kill himself."

"So, you're saying someone murdered him. But who? And how?"

"Figure out how, you'll know who."

Granz paused. "I don't think I like where this conversation seems to be going, Doc."

Nelson shook his head and sighed. "Me, neither. Let's go over the sequence of events again. You said the only time Simmons was alone was when Kate brought you the camera. How long did that take?"

"Maybe ten minutes. She was anxious to get back to Simmons."

"How far was it from the first-class lavatory to your seats?"

"We were in row six at the front of the coach section. There's a partition between first class and coach . . . twelve or fifteen feet."

"Where was Simmons seated?"

"The middle seat in our row."

"Could you see him from the lavatory?"

"No."

Nelson set his coffee on the table in front of the sofa and leaned forward, elbows on his knees.

"Ingested digitalis is absorbed into the bloodstream quickly." His voice was soft, like he was thinking aloud, not talking to Granz. "That's about right."

"What's about right?"

"The only time you, Kate, and Simmons weren't together was when you were securing the lavatory. It takes about ten minutes for a massive digitalis overdose to induce symptoms that mimic a heart attack. Ten minutes after you leave Kate alone with Simmons, he collapses and dies from an apparent heart attack."

Granz froze, coffee cup halfway to his mouth. "You're implying Kathryn murdered Robert Simmons. Jesus Christ, she's my wife!"

"I know, and except for you, the only friend I have in the world."

"Then what the fuck are you doing?"

"Restating the facts, hoping one of us will come up with another explanation. Help me out."

"Kathryn's not capable of murder."

"Under the right circumstances, we're all capable of murder."

"Bullshit!"

"You can't ignore the facts, and the facts say Kathryn may have murdered Robert Simmons."

Granz leaned back on the sofa, silent.

"Dave?" Nelson prompted.

"What th' fuck do I do now, Doc?"

"Your job."

CHAPTER

22

THIS WEEKEND, their first as a married couple, Dave had hoped that he and Kathryn would share the happy news with Emma, then enjoy a special family dinner to celebrate.

Now, he could barely force himself to drive to Kathryn's condo, much less confront her with Morgan Nelson's suspicions about Simmons' murder. Worse, he knew he had to tell her he shared Nelson's concern.

So when he approached her condo complex, instead of pulling into the driveway, he drove around the block four times.

Finally, unable to put it off any longer, he parked in the carport beside her Audi A4. He switched off the V-8, folded the toxicology report, shoved it in his pocket, walked up the stairs, stood on the landing for a few minutes, drew several deep breaths, and punched the doorbell.

"I'll get it!" Dave heard pounding footsteps.

The deadbolt slid open. "*Dave!* I knew it was you." Emma was wearing pajama bottoms and a Holy Cross Middle School sweatshirt, a half-eaten bagel in one hand, a phone in the other.

"Gotta finish dressing, we're going to the mall. Mom's in the kitchen." She gave him a peck on the cheek and ran back to her bedroom, giggling at whoever was on the other end of the phone.

"Who is it, Em?" Kathryn shouted.

Kathryn stood barefoot at the sink, rinsing dishes and loading the dishwasher. She wore Gap jeans and an open-necked blue shirt.

She looked so pretty as his wife that it took Dave's breath away, and he started to put his hands on her shoulders, but changed his mind and stepped back. "It's me, Babe."

She shut the water off, dried her hands, and slipped her arms around his waist. "I told you to be here early so we could sit down with Emma before dinner, but ten A.M.'s overdoing it a little."

"I know."

She smiled mischievously. "You looking for a little affection before lunch?"

"No."

Startled, she leaned back to look at him. "Whatever's on your mind, spill it."

He leaned against the counter and, not knowing how to broach the real issue, explained Nelson's findings from Jemima Tucker's autopsy instead.

"If Keefe or Sanchez left the semen, one or both had sex with her just before or during her murder."

"Or immediately after."

"Yeah, that's a possibility, too. Do we have probable cause to seize their blood for DNA comparison?"

She walked around the breakfast counter, sat on a stool, leaned forward on her elbows and clasped her hands. "PC isn't the problem. The judges are going to circle the wagons around one of their own—conflict out on Keefe, refuse to issue a warrant ordering Keefe to submit to a blood draw."

"Is there an alternative?"

"Grand Juries can issue subpoenas ad testificandum to compel testimony and subpoenas duces tecum to obtain evidence, without probable cause— without even a firm basis for believing the subpoenas will prove the commission of a particular offense."

"Including blood samples?"

"There's conflicting case law, but yes, if the Grand Jury has good reason to believe a crime was committed, and also believes the blood samples will significantly aid its investigation."

"What if they lawyer up to quash the subpoenas?"

"They have a legal right to contest them in court before complying, but I bet they won't. Court hearings are public. By the time they were concluded, it wouldn't matter whether one of them killed Tucker or not, their personal lives and careers would be destroyed."

"How soon can you convene the Grand Jury?"

"The foreperson calls every Monday morning to ask if I have investigations for them. I'll ask them to convene Thursday afternoon at the jail."

The county jail facility contained one secure courtroom, used mostly for arraignments and preliminary hearings for high-risk inmates, and to accommodate overflow from the main court building across the street. "Meanwhile, I'll issue subpoenas for Keefe and Sanchez."

"Why the jail courtroom?"

"So I can have the jail nurse standing by to draw their blood after they testify."

"Good idea," Dave agreed. "Subpoena Bonnie Keefe, too. She disputes Sanchez' alibi that he was having sex with her when Tucker was murdered. Let's get her locked in under oath."

"Will do." She stood. "Now I've got to take Em clothes shopping, then to the grocery store. She doesn't know why, but she suspects tonight's special—we're buying fresh cracked crab, Brie, avocado, French bread, Riesling, and Martinelli's Sparkling Cider for Em. Sound good?"

"We need to talk before dinner, Kate."

"What's going on? If I've done something to make you angry, tell me."

"I'm not angry."

She crossed her arms over her chest, as she always did when protecting herself. "Have you changed your mind about us? Are you sorry we got married? If you are, say so now, before we tell Emma."

He wrapped his arms around her and drew her close. "I love you more than ever, Kathryn. The only thing I'll ever be sorry about is that we didn't have more years together."

"Then what?" She pulled back. "Let's not start the rest of our lives together as a family angry or upset."

He pulled Simmons' tox report out of his pocket and handed it to her. She read it twice.

"This has to be a mistake, it says Simmons died from a digitalis overdose. Simmons didn't carry drugs onto the plane, and he was never out of my sight."

"That's how we saw it." He described his earlier conversation with Morgan Nelson.

Kathryn didn't respond.

"We looked at it from every angle we could figure," he explained, "tried to imagine some other possibility, no matter how far-fetched. After Nelson left, I spent all morning thinking about who had both a motive and an opportunity to murder Simmons."

"And I'm the only person you came up with." She sat down on a stool, her back rigid and her face tight. "That's ridiculous."

"If you tell me you didn't murder Simmons, Kate, I'll believe you."

"I won't dignify this with a denial, and I can't believe you think I'm capable of murder."

"If you won't deny it, how can I not consider the possibility?"

Tears of frustration appeared in the corners of her eyes. She brushed them away angrily, smearing her mascara.

He handed her a second piece of paper, hastily handwritten on Santa Rita County Sheriff's stationery.

"Your resignation?" she asked.

"I don't care if you killed the son of a bitch or not, he deserved it. I should've done it myself. I can't investigate you, you're my wife."

She tore the resignation into pieces and laid them on the countertop. Her hands shook and her voice quivered. "If you don't investigate me, the Attorney General will. I need it to be you."

"If I keep it under wraps, especially now that we're married, it'll look like a cover-up, and that'd be worse for you."

"We have to keep the marriage quiet for a few days, give you time to eliminate me as a suspect."

"We can't conceal it very long."

"It won't take long. I wouldn't expect you to lie about it if someone asks, just don't volunteer."

"Okay, I suppose we don't have any choice."

"What about telling Emma?"

"We can't tell her, then expect her to keep it secret. Let's hold off until I clear up this mess."

CHAPTER

23

"Ms. FOREPERSON, are you ready to proceed?"

"We are."

Mackay faced the elevated oak platform where retired bank manager Nicolina Giacomini presided from the judge's chair. At the court clerk's table beneath the bench, the secretary took roll and noted on his roster that a quorum of sixteen members was present. To her right, remaining jurors occupied the twelve jury-box seats and two alternates' chairs in front.

Inspector Donna Escalante waited outside to admit witnesses as they were called, but besides the jurors, only a court reporter was in the room with Mackay. She wore a classic suit—two-button tweed jacket with notch collar and a straight skirt with back slit. As always, she stood throughout the proceeding.

She placed her hands on the sides of the podium. "Good afternoon, ladies and gentlemen, thank you for convening today. Two weeks ago tomorrow—on the evening of Friday, January eleventh—Superior Court Judge Jemima Tucker was killed in her chambers, here in the main court building. The Sheriff's Crime Scene Investigators found no signs of forced entry to either the court building or to Judge Tucker's chambers, leading investigators to conclude that Judge Tucker knew her murderer."

She paused and made eye contact with each person in the room, most of whom knew Tucker at least slightly from impaneling the Grand Jury, to impress on them the import of her words.

"I asked you to convene for the purpose of conducting an investigation into Judge Tucker's death. Specifically, I ask you to compel the testimony of three witnesses today: Jemima Tucker's husband, Doctor Alejandro Sanchez; Santa Rita Superior Court Judge Reginald Keefe; and Bonnie Lee Keefe, local attorney and wife of Judge Keefe."

She paused while a few of the jurors took notes. "Murder is the unlawful killing of a human being with malice aforethought. The People believe that each of the witnesses who will be called to testify before you here today possesses critical information relevant to the investigation of Judge Tucker's murder."

She waited until the jurors had finished taking notes, then announced, "The People call Doctor Alejandro Sanchez."

The sergeant at arms escorted Sanchez to the witness stand, where he raised his right hand and swore to tell the truth. His jet-black hair was neatly trimmed and combed straight back, he was clean shaven, and he wore an expensive, double-breasted, dark gray wool suit and lightly starched white shirt, with a solid black silk tie. He crossed his right leg over his left, looked at Mackay, and waited.

"Good afternoon, Doctor. Before we begin, I would like to advise you that you are now appearing before a duly constituted Grand Jury which is investigating the murder of Jemima Tucker. Do you understand that?"

"Yes."

"You have been placed under oath and your testimony here today has the same force and effect as if you were in a court of law. Do you understand that?"

"Yes."

"That means that you have an obligation to tell the truth in the proceeding or you could subject yourself to a possible prosecution for perjury. Do you understand that?"

"Yes."

"Finally, you are advised that under the Fifth Amendment of the Constitution of the United States, and also under Article I of the California Constitution, that you have a privilege against self-incrimination. That is to say, you do not have to answer any questions which may tend to incriminate you, or subject you to punishment for any crime, and that you can refuse to answer any such question, stating that the answer may tend to incriminate you. Do you understand?"

Sanchez uncrossed and recrossed his legs. "Yes, I understand."

"If you have retained counsel, the Grand Jury will permit you a reasonable opportunity to step outside the room to consult with counsel if you do so desire. State your name, please."

"Alejandro Sanchez."

"What is your business or occupation?"

"I'm an emergency room physician at Española Community Hospital." Sanchez' voice was barely audible.

"I realize this is difficult, Doctor, but please speak loudly enough for the reporter to record your answers." Mackay softened her voice. "You were married to Jemima Tucker?"

"Yes."

"Would you characterize your marriage as happy or unhappy?"

"I don't know how to answer that."

"Were you aware that your wife had consulted with a divorce lawyer?"

"My attorney told me not to answer questions about my relationship with my wife."

"As I previously stated, the Grand Jury is investigating the murder of your deceased wife. Are you refusing to answer questions about your relationship on the grounds that *truthful* answers would tend to incriminate you?"

"I didn't say that."

"Well, Doctor, that is the only grounds for refusing to answer my questions without being held in contempt of court."

"I'd like to consult with my attorney."

Mackay and the jurors waited for several minutes. When Sanchez returned, Mackay repeated the question.

"On advice of counsel, I refuse to answer," Sanchez stated.

"Very well. You told us that you work in the emergency room at Española Community Hospital. What hours do you normally work?"

"It varies. ER doctors rotate monthly. We generally work twenty-four-hour shifts starting at noon one day and ending at noon the next."

"Were you working last January eleventh?"

"Yes, I went to work at noon."

"And worked straight through until noon the next day—Saturday, the twelfth?"

"That's correct."

"During your twenty-four-hour shifts, do you normally eat your meals on the hospital premises?"

"I . . . Yes, normally."

"On the evening of January eleventh, did you eat dinner at the hospital?"

Sanchez uncrossed his legs and leaned forward. "On advice of counsel, I refuse to answer."

"All right. Do you recall meeting with Sheriff Granz and me on the Sunday immediately following your wife's death?"

"Yes."

"During that interview, did you tell us that you left the hospital for a little over an hour at about six o'clock, during which you were engaged in sexual intercourse with Bonnie Keefe?"

"On advice of counsel, I refuse to answer."

"Are you aware, Doctor, that Ms. Keefe has denied being with you that evening?"

"No! I . . . On advice of counsel, I refuse to answer."

"Is there *any* question I could ask you having to do with your wife, Jemima Tucker, or January eleventh that you would *not* refuse to answer, Doctor?"

"Probably not."

"Thank you, Doctor, you are dismissed. However, under penalty of contempt, you must appear before this Grand Jury at some later time, if requested to do so. Inspector Escalante is standing by outside to escort you to the jail nurse, who will take a sample of your blood."

When Sanchez left, Giacomini asked, "Ms. Mackay, how should we interpret his refusal to answer your questions?"

Mackay partially turned to face the jury box. "Good question. The Fifth Amendment privilege not only extends to answers that would in themselves support a conviction under California law, but likewise embraces those that would furnish a link in the chain of evidence needed to prosecute the murderer of Judge Tucker. I apologize for being so formal, but that is the proper legal terminology. In everyday vernacular, it means that a truthful answer might furnish, or lead to, evidence that could be used against him."

"It doesn't necessarily mean he killed her, though, right?"

"That would be up to a trial jury to decide, if he were charged with murder and prosecuted. Are there any other questions?"

The jurors all shook their heads. "The People call Judge Reginald Keefe."

Keefe was neither cooperative nor intimidated. As soon as he was sworn, he sat in the witness chair and glared a challenge at Mackay, who advised him of his rights exactly as she had Sanchez. He stated that he understood.

"State your name, please," she directed.

"Reginald Keefe. *Judge* Reginald Keefe."

"You are a Santa Rita County Superior Court Judge?"

"You know the answer to that question."

"Please answer for the record."

"I'm a Superior Court Judge."

"Were you acquainted with Judge Jemima Tucker?"

"Of course."

"How long had you known Judge Tucker before her death?"

"Ten years, maybe longer. I was already a judge when she was appointed to the bench, I believe it was ten or eleven years ago."

"Eleven. How *well* did you know Jemima Tucker?"

Keefe started to speak, then stopped. "As well as one can know a colleague with whom he works and consults closely over many years. She was a gifted lawyer and jurist."

"Did you meet with Judge Tucker privately, in her chambers or yours?"

"Where else would we meet?"

"Is that a 'yes'?"

"Yes."

"Did you meet with Judge Tucker in her chambers or yours before court convened in the morning, during lunch breaks, or after normal working hours, when court staff had gone home?"

For the first time, Keefe's gaze wavered. He glanced down and picked an imaginary fleck of lint off his trousers, then looked up. "Sometimes."

"Frequently?"

"Is this going someplace, Ms. Mackay? I was forced to cancel my afternoon calendar to appear before the Grand Jury. I am pleased to cooperate, but this isn't the only matter that requires judicial attention."

Mackay ignored the sarcasm, but before repeating the question, said, "For the record, yesterday you sought an ex parte stay of this Grand Jury investigation, which was rejected by the presiding judge, citing confidentiality of these proceedings. I suggest you cooperate more fully, Judge, or you'll find yourself in front of that same judge facing a contempt hearing."

The witness hesitated briefly, then answered, "I suppose one might say we met frequently."

"Daily?"

"Sometimes."

"More than once a day?"

"Sometimes."

"Is it common for judges to meet privately in chambers every day?"

"You'd have to ask the other judges."

"I shall. So, you knew Judge Tucker well, at least as a colleague. Did you know her well in any capacity other than as a colleague?"

Keefe stared at Mackay. "Be specific."

"Did you socialize?"

"There are only a dozen judges in the county. For reasons I'm sure are apparent to you, judges rarely socialize outside their own small circle. My wife and I socialized with Judge Tucker and Doctor Sanchez on many occasions, as we did with all the judges and their spouses."

Mackay nodded and placed her hand on her chin, as if thinking of the next question. "Did you and Judge Tucker socialize in private, just the two of you, either on or off the court-building premises?"

Keefe stared for several seconds, straightened his tie, interlaced his fingers and clenched them in his lap, then cleared his throat. "I refuse to answer that question on the grounds that my answer might tend to incriminate me, as I shall refuse to answer any more questions pertaining to my professional or personal relationship with Jemima—Judge Tucker."

"You are aware that Fifth Amendment rights can only be asserted as to testimony on a question-by-question basis, and not as a blanket refusal to answer questions before they have been asked?"

"I am aware of that, Ms. Mackay, but it would save a lot of time."

"The grand jurors and I prefer to hear each of your responses. Perhaps I will stumble across a question about your relationship with Jemima Tucker to which you *don't* think a *truthful* answer would incriminate you."

Keefe leaned back in the witness chair and folded

his arms over his chest in defiance. "Then, go ahead. Ask your questions and waste our time."

"Thank you." Mackay looked at the court reporter. "Please read back my last question."

She unfolded several sheets of tape. "'Did you and Judge Tucker socialize in private, just the two of you, either on or off the court-building premises?'"

"I refuse to answer on the grounds that my answer might tend to incriminate me."

"On Thursday, January tenth, the day before she was killed, did you and Jemima Tucker walk to lunch together across the footbridge from the park to the theater? And, during that walk, did you and Jemima Tucker kiss twice?"

Keefe blanched visibly, then he rose from his chair. His face turned red, and spittle accumulated in the corners of his mouth. "Dammit, that's enough! Don't you have any respect, any common decency? Jemima's dead, for God's sake!"

Mackay saw tears form in Keefe's eyes, so she took three steps to her left, intentionally directing his face away from the jury box, and said softly, "Please sit down, Judge, so it isn't necessary to call Inspector Escalante."

He slowly settled into the chair, pulled a tissue from the box on the railing around the witness chair, held it over his nose, and pretended to sneeze.

"Take your time," Mackay said, not unkindly.

He wadded up the tissue and leaned forward so his elbows rested on the railing. "I refuse to answer on the grounds that my answer might tend to incriminate me."

"One last question, Judge Keefe. Did you engage in sexual intercourse with Jemima Tucker within seventy-two hours of her murder?"

Keefe's lips moved, but nothing came out.

"I didn't hear your answer, Judge."

"I refuse to answer on the grounds that my answer might tend to incriminate me."

The room was silent. Mackay glanced around and noted that all the jurors avoided eye contact, as if they felt and were somehow responsible for Reginald Keefe's pain and embarrassment.

"Thank you, Judge, you are dismissed. But remember that under penalty of contempt, you might be required to appear before this Grand Jury at a later time. Please contact Inspector Escalante when you leave, so the jail nurse can take your blood sample."

Keefe started to object, changed his mind, then walked slowly from the room.

"Does anyone want to take a short break?" Mackay asked. Seeing that no one did, she announced, "The People call Bonnie Lee Keefe."

Bonnie Keefe's presence was palpable. She wore a tightly tailored beige suit with a skirt that ended above her knees, and a chocolate-brown silk blouse one size too small. She crossed the room, raised her hand, and swore to tell the truth. Then, before sitting in the witness chair, she unbuttoned her suit coat, slipped it off, and folded it over the railing, emphasizing what male jurors undoubtedly considered her best features.

"Before we begin," Mackay said, "I would like to advise you that you are now appearing before a duly constituted Grand Jury which is investigating a violation of state criminal law. You have been placed under oath and your testimony here today has the same force and effect as if you were in a court of law. That means that you have an obligation to tell the truth in the proceeding or you could subject yourself to a possible prosecution for perjury. Do you understand?"

"Yes."

"I also want to advise you that based on information we now possess, there is no expectation or intention, at this time, of seeking any charges against you personally as a result of that investigation. Do you understand that?"

"I understand."

"State your name, please."

"Bonnie Lee Keefe."

"What is your business or occupation?"

"I'm a civil litigator."

"You're married to Judge Reginald Keefe?"

"I am."

"Were you acquainted with Judge Jemima Tucker?"
"Yes."

"And her husband, Doctor Alejandro Sanchez?"
She hesitated almost imperceptibly. "Yes."

"How well did you know them?"

"We were friends."

"How did you learn of Judge Tucker's death?"

"You and Sheriff Granz came to our home . . ." she glanced upward as she tried to remember, "around midnight, as I recall, on January eleventh, to ask my husband—Judge Keefe—to sign a search warrant. It was for the Tucker home. That was the first I heard about it."

"What was your and Judge Keefe's reaction on hearing that your friend had been murdered?"

"We were both shocked."

"Do you recall on the following Monday, January fourteenth, being interviewed by Sheriff's Chief of Detectives Miller and DA Inspector Escalante with respect to Judge Tucker's death?"

"Yes, they came to my office that morning."

"And at that time, as you have just stated, you were already aware that Jemima Tucker had been killed?"

"Yes."

Mackay opened a file folder and placed her hands on the podium. "I have Detective Miller's report here, Mrs. Keefe. Please tell us, to the best of your recollection, the substance of that interview."

"They asked if I was acquainted with Judge Tucker and her husband. I said I knew them both. Then they asked whether or not I had been with Doctor Sanchez on the evening of January eleventh."

"What did you say?"

"I said 'no.' "

"Did they tell you Doctor Sanchez claimed to have been engaged in sexual intercourse with you at your office, from sometime after six P.M. until sometime before seven-thirty P.M. on Friday, January eleventh— approximately the time Judge Tucker was killed?"

"Yes."

"Did they ask if that was true?"

"Yes."

"What did you tell them?"

"That I was not with Doctor Sanchez at that time."

Mackay stepped around the podium and moved very slowly toward the witness. "Thank you. Now, Mrs. Keefe, can you please confirm under oath that you were not with Doctor Sanchez on the evening of January eleventh?"

"No." Bonnie Lee sat up straight and looked directly at Mackay. "I am, however, willing to modify the statements I originally made to Detective Miller and Inspector Escalante, providing I am not subject to prosecution or other sanction for giving a false statement."

Mackay stopped and considered the bomb that had just dropped. "I am granting you use immunity; therefore, your testimony here today cannot be used to prove you made false statements to investigators. However, you must testify truthfully before this Grand Jury."

"I understand." She drew a deep breath and expelled it slowly. "The investigators took me by complete surprise. For me to admit being involved in a sexual relationship outside of marriage would have devastated Judge Keefe. I wasn't thinking clearly."

"Well, if you are thinking clearly now, Mrs. Keefe, tell us where you were from approximately six P.M. until seven-thirty P.M. on the evening of Friday, January eleventh."

"I was at my law office."

"Engaged in sexual intercourse with Doctor Alejandro Sanchez?"

"Yes."

CHAPTER

24

"MORNING, MS. MACKAY. Your usual?" The young woman at the Starbucks cart in the court-building atrium held a paper cup under the Sumatra spigot.

"Yeah, thanks. I thought you didn't work Fridays." She dropped the change from her two dollars into the tip jar.

"I don't usually, but we're on winter break. One more semester and I'll be finished."

Mackay sipped her coffee through the hole in the plastic lid. "What are your plans after Portola Community College?"

"I've been accepted to Cal Poly's agricultural engineering program. The only woman this year."

"Congratulations, Marcie. I'll miss you."

"Dad says he plans to rent out my bedroom."

"I'm sure he's joking."

"Hope so."

"I dread the day when Emma . . ."

She was interrupted by the chirp of her cell phone. She waved to Marcie, walked to a vacant concrete bench, set the coffee down, and dug her phone from her handbag.

"Mackay."

"Dan Burford here."

Mackay recognized the County Counsel's high, almost feminine voice. "Hi, Dan."

"We need to meet," he said abruptly.

"Sure. How about tomorrow morning, nine o'clock?"

A silence on the other end of the line was followed by the sound of Burford covering the mouthpiece with his hand, then muffled voices.

"This can't wait. My conference room—five minutes?" It was more an order than a request.

Mackay frowned. "Okay."

A long, skinny, rectangular ex-storage space whose metal door barely fit one of the two smaller walls, the County Counsel conference room was also a law library and employee lounge. Furnished with only a beat-up oak table and a dozen mismatched chairs, and lacking natural light or ventilation, its stale air smelled of sweaty bodies, musty old paper, and overripe coffee.

Supervisor Philip Boynton sat farthest from the door at the head of the table, Supervisor Janet Gutierrez to his left, County Administrative Officer Sharon Brice to his right with a stack of papers on the table in front of her, and Burford beside Brice. When Mackay entered, they looked up and nodded, but didn't speak. Burford indicated for Mackay to be seated at the foot of the table by the door.

Mackay hesitated, then swung the door shut. "What's going on? This feels like an inquisition."

"Then I'll get right to the point," Boynton said.

Boynton and Gutierrez supported her ex-Chief Deputy Neal McCaskill, whom she had fired soon after taking office, when he opposed her first reelection campaign. Mackay won the acrimonious race by a large majority, and had since declared a cautious truce with the two Supervisors.

McCaskill went into private practice, but as a regular columnist for the local newspaper, he continually criticized her administration, often levying totally unfounded charges.

She leaned forward to rest her forearms on the table and clasped her hands. "I'm listening."

"We've learned that Doctor Robert Simmons did *not* suffer a heart attack during the flight from Spain to San Francisco. We also know that an investigation into his murder has been launched, and that the investigation has focused on you as the prime suspect."

Mackay raised her hands, palms out, as if to push away an intruder. "Where did you get that information?"

"Doesn't matter. Do you deny it?"

"Damn right I deny it. I didn't murder Simmons."

"That remains to be seen. What I meant was, do you deny you're the focus of that investigation?"

"Ask the Sheriff."

"We did, early this morning, and we've made a decision."

"What decision?"

Boynton glanced around the room. "To demand that you resign immediately."

Mackay stared at each person. Only Burford held her gaze. "Who the hell is 'we'?"

"The Board of Supervisors."

"Without posting an agenda and holding a public hearing, the Board couldn't make that decision unless it met illegally, in secret. If so, I'll prosecute every person who attended that meeting, including you, your CAO, and County Counsel."

"We've committed no illegal acts that you can prove."

"We'll see about that."

"A majority of the Board demands your immediate resignation until you are exonerated, if that is the outcome of the Simmons investigation."

Boynton pulled a document from his briefcase and passed it to Mackay. "Your official resignation. We expect you to sign and submit it before you leave this room."

Mackay started to read it, but changed her mind, wadded it up, and dropped it on the floor.

"I refuse. The voters elected me to be their District Attorney, and unless they remove me, I intend to do my job."

She pushed back her chair. "Now, if you're finished with this nonsense, I have work waiting."

"Please hear us out," Boynton said.

"Make it fast."

Brice slid her stack of papers to Mackay. "These are recall petitions, ready to be circulated and filed. You can see they already contain several signatures. If they fail, I'll file suit."

"On what legal grounds?"

"I'm not sure yet, but it won't matter. Even if I lose the case, your career'll be over."

"Considering your large margin of victory at the polls," Boynton interjected, "the Board won't survive a public confrontation with you undamaged. We know that. But the one thing that would be worse for us, knowing what we do now, would be to do nothing. If that became public—and it would—we'd be tarred and feathered. We plan to preempt such an occurrence."

She swallowed the bitter bile that rose in her throat. "I've been a successful litigator for more than twenty years. If you repeat what you said to anyone outside this room, or if you circulate those petitions, you'll have a war on your hands."

"Be reasonable, Kathryn," Burford said. "If you refuse to step down while you're under investigation, every conviction your office wins will be tainted. They'll go up on appeal, be reversed, and have to be retried. It'll bring the criminal justice system in Santa Rita to its knees for years."

"I won't resign just to make it easy for everyone else."

"Will you discuss an alternative that'll make it easier for all of us, including yourself?" Boynton asked.

"Such as?"

"The Board will place you on paid administrative

leave until the investigation is concluded, one way or the other."

"That'd make me look guilty."

"We'll issue a statement to the press signed by all five Supervisors, stating that out of concern for your office and the public, you came to us and suggested that you take a leave of absence without pay."

"What a crock!"

He ignored her. "Our statement will make it clear that we insisted you accept full pay and benefits until you're cleared of all charges, which we are confident will happen swiftly, at which time you will resume office."

The strength seemed to drain from Mackay's body. She sat back and put her hands in her lap, gripping them tightly together to stop the trembling. "If I don't agree?"

"Then we'd have no choice. The CAO will submit the recall petitions to the Elections Department, and County Counsel will file his Superior Court action by the end of the day."

"I suppose you've already drafted an agreement for me to sign."

Burford handed her a final sheet of paper. "We tried to anticipate all the possibilities and make it as easy for you as possible."

Mackay sat silently, considering her options. "Before I sign this, I need to tell my Chief Deputy, Mary Elizabeth Skinner, personally. And appoint her Interim DA."

Boynton shook his head. "No. If you accept—and this is not negotiable—we make the appointment."

"No one else is qualified."

"There's one experienced, highly qualified person outside your office who could assume the position seamlessly, without being perceived as your clone, or a mere rubber stamp for your policies. He's agreed to accept the interim appointment."

Mackay signed the agreement, snapped the cover on her pen, and replaced it in her bag. "Who?"

"Neal McCaskill."

CHAPTER

25

THE DOJ LAB looked like the FedEx building next door: clean, modern, utilitarian, and nondescript. Unlike the other commercial buildings on Research Drive, though, it backed up against a grassy hillside with a view of the bay that by itself could have converted a $250,000 fixer-upper into a $4 million rustic estate.

In his late forties, short, and overweight, Neal McCaskill combed his thinning hair over his bald spot and plastered it down with a heavy layer of hair spray. He wore a high-priced winter suit under a slate-gray London Fog topcoat. He was leaning against his Lexus GS430 when Sheriff Granz pulled his Buick into the parking lot, climbed out, and walked over.

"We going to have any problems?" McCaskill asked unceremoniously.

"What the hell does that mean?"

"Are you gonna give me a hard time, or will you work with me as District Attorney?"

"*Interim* District Attorney," Granz corrected. "You could've asked me that on the phone."

"I wanted to watch your eyes."

Granz poked his forefinger at McCaskill's chest. "I didn't like you when we both worked for Benton, and I don't like you now."

"Breaks my heart. So, what's your answer?"

"I'll do my job, make sure you do yours."

"Count on it."

"Then we understand each other." Granz turned and headed to the lab's main entrance. "Why did you ask me to meet you here?"

McCaskill followed, his short pudgy legs churning fast to keep up with Granz' long strides. "DOJ has the DNA results on the Tucker rape kit."

"How'd you find out?"

"I'm District Attorney. I called 'em because I didn't want the results to get lost somewhere between your office and mine."

"Don't unpack the moving cartons. Like I said, you're only an Interim."

At the door they were met by a uniformed security guard with white hair. "Hi, Sheriff."

"How's retirement, Richard?"

"Better'n poundin' a beat in the Tenderloin, and I don't have to commute to San Francisco."

"We're here to see Menendez."

"Good timing, she just got back from lunch."

They signed in, then walked across the lobby to a heavy metal door, where the guard punched in a security code. The door swung open to reveal a tiny, sterile anteroom where criminalist Roselba Menendez waited.

Like her crime-lab colleagues, she worked in casual clothes—jeans, a Pacific Cookie Company T-shirt, and white Reeboks. She looked like any other pretty young woman, but she was the best criminalist Granz knew.

She led them past a waist-high swinging gate into a narrow hallway lined with unmarked steel doors. Most were closed, but a few stood ajar, exposing an array of scientific equipment. She stopped at the last door, punched in a security code, and swung it open into a large, open office crammed with desks, chairs, computers, and filing cabinets. She slid two metal stools to a stainless steel bench and motioned them to sit.

"We've completed typing the STRs," she told them.

McCaskill unconsciously scratched his head, mussing his stiff hair, causing it to stick up like a rooster's comb. "What happened to typing RLFPs?"

Granz snorted. "You've been outta the scientific loop too long, McCaskill. Restriction fragment length polymorphism typing went out with dinosaurs and AquaNet in aerosol cans."

"Oh. Is that what RFLP stands for?"

Menendez suppressed a smile, but sensed McCaskill's embarrassment. She reached over and smoothed his hair.

"Sheriff's right," she confirmed. "The main shortcoming of RFLP was that it required large biological samples. That led us to polymerase chain reaction, an advancement enabling us to analyze much smaller crime-scene samples by duplicating the DNA before typing. That led to what we do now—an automated analysis called short tandem repeats."

McCaskill started to scratch again, caught himself, and tucked his hands in his pants pockets. "Isn't RFLP typing preferred because it's highly discriminating?"

"Yes, but luckily, STR analysis is as discriminating as RFLP, and has other benefits as well."

"Such as?"

"Mainly, it's faster and cheaper. RFLP was a manual procedure, which meant we had to wait five to six weeks for results. STRs are amenable to automation, so we can achieve a twenty-four-hour turnaround when necessary."

"Obviously, I don't know much, but I feel still most comfortable with RFLP, it's been around a long time."

"RFLP's obsolete science, and STR's been used since the early nineties."

"Yeah?"

"The Feds used it first to ID remains of Desert Storm soldiers. In '93, they used it to identify the Branch Davidian victims in Texas, then the bodies from the TWA's Flight 800 crash. Most recently they used it at Ground Zero and the Pentagon. It's a well-established typing procedure."

"RFLP's already admissible in court."

"True, you'll probably have to put on an admissibility hearing before you're allowed to present the results, but I can help you with that."

Granz laughed. "Better start now, I think our *Interim* DA needs some basic lessons on prosecuting a DNA case."

McCaskill took a step toward Granz. "Kiss off."

"Maybe a little primer *is* in order, Mr. McCaskill," Menendez suggested, stepping between them.

McCaskill was relieved to be saved the indignity of backing down. "Shoot."

"After DNA is extracted from the biological sample, the technician amplifies, or copies, it using the PCR procedure, which chemically amplifies a sample that's too small or degraded for RFLP typing. Fluorescent dye is then introduced to mark the beginning and end of each target STR sequence, and to label that DNA section. The labeled products are copied, separated by a special gel, zapped with a laser to establish the genetic profile, and finally printed out as a graph called an electropherogram."

"How do you determine if there's a match or not?"

"By comparing the electropherograms from several loci. STRs are scattered throughout the human genome, and while a match at one STR loci isn't conclusive, a genetic profile from several STR loci will discriminate conclusively between any two individuals except identical twins."

"Jesus! I'll just subpoena you and let you explain that scientific mumbo-jumbo to the jury, rather than waste my valuable time trying to sort it out. Bottom line—did you get a match from Tucker's rape kit?"

"One. The DNA profile from the vaginal swab matches the profile from Judge Keefe's blood standard. It was his semen."

"How sweet—two judges boffing each other in chambers and now it looks like one of 'em's a murder suspect. How about her husband?"

Menendez shot McCaskill a dirty look. "Doctor Sanchez is excluded as donor of the semen on both the vaginal *and* the anal swabs."

"Oh, that's just great. Can you people tell me who shot the semen up Tucker's ass, or do I have to use my imagination?"

Menendez' olive complexion gave way to a deep red blush. "That's for you to find out, Mr. McCaskill."

McCaskill started to walk away, then stopped and turned. "I thought that's what you were paid to do. I guess I'm on my own."

As he headed to the door, Menendez stared at his retreating back, then flipped him the finger.

"Shoulda left the little jerk's hair sticking up so he looks as stupid as he acts," she told Granz.

Granz smiled. "Next time."

"Next time, come by yourself."

Granz patted her on the shoulder. "My pleasure."

CHAPTER

26

GRANZ AND MCCASKILL LEANED against Granz'
Buick.

McCaskill smoothed his hair. "Where does that
leave our investigation into Tucker's murder?"

"It isn't *our* investigation, it's mine."

"The protocol is for the Sheriff to keep the District
Attorney informed."

"I know the drill, McCaskill, so don't create any
territorial disputes with me. It's *my* investigation
until I turn it over to you for prosecution. In the
meantime, I make the decisions, including what
information you get. Now, get off my car, I've got to
get back to my office."

"There's one other thing."

"What?"

"The Simmons murder."

"I don't know for certain that he was murdered. He could have intentionally overdosed to avoid a trial."

"That's a crock of bull, and you know it."

"Even if he was, I don't know who murdered him."

"Yes, you do, and so do I. I knew you couldn't keep your personal feelings from overriding your professional obligations. I stopped by the morgue on the way here, talked to Nelson. Take Mackay into custody."

"Don't have probable cause."

McCaskill laughed. "You've made hundreds of arrests with a lot less PC. Arrest her ass."

"Fuck you."

"Then I'll bust her myself."

Granz pushed away from the car, turned toward McCaskill, and clenched his fists. "Stay away from Kathryn or . . ."

"Or what? If you're too pussy-whipped to do your job, I'll do it for you. Just stay out of my way."

CHAPTER
27

"Mom, what are you doing here?"

"I thought I'd give you a ride home from soccer practice."

"Ashley and I were going to walk home together."

"I need to talk to you, honey. It's important."

Emma tossed her books into the backseat of the Audi A4. "Can we go by Sophia's and get a burrito? I'm hungry."

Kathryn merged into traffic. "It's only four o'clock. Didn't you eat lunch?"

"Yeah, but that was a long time ago. Can we?"

"I suppose we can pick something up and take it home. We've got to eat dinner anyway, and I don't feel like cooking."

Emma gave her mother a long look. "You said you

have something important to talk to me about. Am I in big trouble?"

Kathryn patted her daughter's knee. "Of course not."

"You've been crying."

"What makes you think that?"

"Your mascara's all streaked."

"Oh."

"What's wrong?"

"Let's talk about it at home, okay?"

Emma rode in silence for several minutes, then asked, "It's bad, isn't it?"

"I know you're anxious, but please, let's wait until we get home."

She turned into the small shopping center where Sophia's Taqueria occupied an inconspicuous rear space, dug in her purse, pulled out her cell phone and a wadded-up twenty-dollar bill, and handed the cash to Emma. "Would you mind getting our food while I make a phone call?"

"Sure. Plain quesadilla with a side order of guacamole, right?"

"You know me so well." Kathryn tried to smile, but it turned out to be a grimace, which Emma noticed.

"You should talk to me about what's bothering you now. I love you, and I'm a good listener, you know."

Kathryn felt tears well up again, but willed them to stop, then leaned over and kissed her daughter's cheek.

"I know you are, Em, and you can't imagine how

important that is to me right now. But run along and get the food so I can make my call."

Kathryn had spent most of the day sitting alone in her car parked near the beach, unable to think of how to tell a young girl that her mother was a murder suspect. But she needed to break the news soon to avoid Emma hearing it first on the evening news or, worse, from a girlfriend who called to ask about it.

She tried to contact Dave Granz several times, but he was out of his office. His secretary said she'd heard the news. She had just hung up from another unsuccessful attempt when Emma returned.

They drove home silently. As she pulled the car into the driveway of her condo, Emma said, "Mom, there are some men in a car parked in front of our carport."

"Yes, I see."

The unmarked Ford Taurus backed into her parking space belonged to the DA Inspectors' motor pool. When the two men in the car spotted her, they started to open the doors.

Kathryn zipped into an empty parking space, shut off the engine, and climbed out.

"Take the food inside, Em, I need to talk with these men for a minute."

"Mom, I'm scared."

"They're from my office, honey." Kathryn gave Emma a hug. "Everything's all right, I promise. But please go inside now."

Kathryn watched until Emma was inside, then turned to face DA Chief of Inspectors James Fields and Neal McCaskill.

McCaskill had buttoned his coat against the cold, causing his jowls to hang over the collar.

Stocky and dark with a face that bore the aftermath of teenage acne, Fields wore only a suit that was damp and wrinkled. The right sleeve of his coat was gathered and tucked into itself where his right hand had been before a bomb blew up a courtroom and his hand years before. After months of intense rehabilitation that taught him to shoot left-handed, he had been restored to full duty as a DA Inspector. One of Kathryn's first acts as DA was to appoint him Chief of her Inspectors Division. He had rewarded her with quiet competence, dogged determination, and fierce loyalty.

McCaskill walked ahead of Fields, stopping with his pudgy face just inches from Mackay's. "You're under arrest for the murder of Robert Simmons."

"You can't arrest me without a warrant."

"I have a warrant. I think Judge Keefe rather enjoyed signing it."

She looked at Fields. "Is this for real?"

"I'm afraid so."

McCaskill grabbed her upper arm. "Turn around, Mackay." He looked at Fields. "Cuff her."

"Jesus Christ, Mac, that's not necessary."

"DA's policy. She's a felon."

She struggled to break free. "You bastard, let me go," she demanded.

"You're not going anyplace except Blaine Street." McCaskill sneered at the mention of the women's detention facility. "Now, turn around so he can cuff you, or I'll do it myself."

She turned her back. Fields snicked the handcuffs loosely on her wrists, then opened the front passenger door of the car and helped her sit.

"What about my daughter?"

McCaskill held the passenger door open and leaned inside. "Fields'll book you into jail. As soon as I get back to my office, I'll send Child Protective Services to take her into custody."

"Dammit, wait with her! She's only twelve years old. You can't leave her alone."

"Should've thought of that before you murdered Simmons."

CHAPTER

28

MACKAY WAITED until Fields started the engine. "You can't let some CPS worker show up and take Emma into custody. She'll be terrified."

"I know." Fields pulled the car out of the driveway, drove around the corner, then stopped at the curb, switched off the engine, and pulled a key ring from his pocket.

"Had to get out of McCaskill's sight. Turn around so I can take off those damn cuffs." He unlocked the handcuffs and dropped them on the seat, then picked up his cell phone. "I'll call Dave to pick Emma up."

"I tried a few minutes ago. He didn't answer."

"Then I'll call Shirley, have her drive Emma to our house."

"No, if you and your wife get involved, McCaskill

will fire you, and I need you there on the inside. Let me call Ruth. She can take Em upstairs to her place before CPS shows up."

Fields handed her the phone. After more than ten years of being called on short notice, Ruth wasn't surprised when Mackay was called out, and, as Emma's self-appointed surrogate grandmother, she welcomed the opportunities. Ruth suggested that Emma spend the night with her, and Mackay gratefully agreed without saying why.

She handed the phone back to Fields. "I . . . Thanks." It came out as a partial sob. "I'm sorry."

"If you need to cry, go ahead."

"If I start crying I won't make it through this." She drew a deep breath, blew it out forcefully and straightened her back. "Let's get it over with."

"Not yet." Fields opened the glove box and pulled out the hidden radio mike. Maybe I can raise Dave on the squawk box. "S-O One, this is D-A-I One."

A metallic voice crackled back through the cheap under-dash speaker: "Granz."

"Go to C channel." Fields rotated the radio knob to switch to a scrambled channel.

Momentarily, Granz came back on. "What's up, Jim?"

"Dave, I have Kathryn Mackay in custody."

"You what!"

"McCaskill got Keefe to sign a warrant and arrested her for Simmons' murder. I'm transporting her to jail."

"That son of a bitch! Put Kathryn on."

Fields handed the mike to Mackay.

"You all right, Babe?" Granz asked.

"Except for being scared, I think so. I tried to call you all day." She paused. "I'm sure glad to hear your voice."

"I had no idea this was coming, that asshole McCaskill never said a word about it. I'm sorry I wasn't there for you."

Fields shouted toward the mike, "Where are you now?"

"Just entering the Santa Rita city limits."

"What should I do? McCaskill ordered me to book Kathryn, then be at the DA's office to poly Keefe at six o'clock."

The radio was silent for several seconds before Granz responded. "Take the long route to the jail. I'll meet you there in thirty minutes and handle the booking myself."

"Commute traffic's pretty heavy. See you in half an hour."

CHAPTER

29

FIELDS PARKED NEXT TO GRANZ' BUICK behind the women's detention facility on Blaine Street, switched off the windshield wipers, and killed the engine. A closed-circuit camera followed them up the broad, floodlighted concrete ramp that led from the wet parking lot to the rear of the building. He stopped at the top of the landing.

"Ready?"

"Ready as I'll ever be."

He nodded, and punched a button. A buzzer sounded and the deadbolt slammed open to release the spring-loaded metal security door that accessed a small concrete room. Fields dropped his Glock 9mm pistol into a built-in drawer, slid it shut, pocketed the key, and punched a second button.

When the inner door opened, Dave Granz walked over and put his arms around Mackay. She held him for several seconds, then pulled away. "Can we get this over with? If I'm going to jail, I need to get used to it."

"You aren't going to spend any time in jail."

"I don't understand."

"By the time my detention officer fingerprints you and takes your photograph, your bail will have been posted. I'll be with you the whole time."

"McCaskill didn't give me time to arrange bail."

"Course not. But I know a bail bondsman. It's taken care of."

"The bail schedule's half a million. Where'd you come up with the fifty-thousand-dollar deposit?"

"Put up my house. Where's Emma?"

"At Ruth's."

"Good, she doesn't have to know about this. Let's get it done and go home."

CHAPTER

30

"WHERE DO MURDER SUSPECTS usually sit?" Reginald Keefe's laugh emphasized his nervousness.

"Anyplace they want." Fields booted up the LX Polygraph Software on his Lafayette LX3000 computerized polygraph and connected the Compaq Presario laptop.

"I can move my equipment wherever you're most comfortable."

"No place would be comfortable." Keefe glanced around the conference room-law library that connected the DA's inner offices to the second-floor hallway. Twelve chairs surrounded the blond oak table, one at each end and five on either side. He sat at the head of the table.

"I came directly from court." He loosened his gray necktie, unbuttoned his shirt collar, and ran his fingers over his five o'clock shadow. "It's been a long, unpleasant day."

"I'll make it as fast and tolerable as possible."

"I've never taken a lie detector test before."

"I have, during my certification training, and I know what an ordeal it is. That's why I'll explain everything as many times as you want, so you understand exactly what's happening."

"When does the test start?"

"Already did. This part's the pre-interview, when I explain things and answer *your* questions."

Fields slid his machine to the end of the table and sat down, then handed Keefe a piece of paper. "A copy of the questions. You're entitled to know exactly what you'll be asked."

"Before you ask?"

"Right. I'll ask the questions on that paper, and *only* these questions, in exactly the order they're listed. There'll be no surprises. No trick questions. We'll rehearse the questions and answers as many times as you want, so you get used to them, before the machine is attached."

Keefe read them carefully. "Why so few questions?"

"Professional guidelines limit a polygrapher to no more than sixteen questions during an examination. In your case, that many aren't necessary."

Keefe pointed at the machine. "Explain those wires, tubes, and other gizmos."

"When a person is asked a question about a specific event, such as Judge Tucker's murder, he consciously decides to tell the truth or lie. If he's truthful, his body goes about its normal biological business. But, a decision to lie induces anxiety that changes various autonomic functions."

"Like?"

"Sweat-gland activity increases; muscles twitch; the heart can skip a beat; blood volume changes; blood pressure increases or decreases. Sensors measure changes that the polygraph records, and plots on a graph."

"I have high blood pressure, and being nervous probably caused it to shoot through the roof."

"You'd be abnormal if you weren't nervous. But it won't affect the test, or make you look guilty, because my analysis will take that into account."

"Explain the analysis."

"I use a software program called AP Polyscore 4.0 to evaluate your charts against known biological patterns, based on algorithms developed by Johns Hopkins University. It takes into account your baseline responses, which I'll establish at the start of the test by asking you a few easy questions."

"What questions?"

"Your name, age, what you do for a living, and so forth."

"How reliable is this?"

"The federal government and several independent universities studied almost three hundred specific-issue investigations like this one. The accuracy rate exceeded ninety-five percent."

"It's the five percent I worry about. How can I be sure you interpret my responses correctly?"

"Good question. At the end of the test, you can explain any questionable or unusual responses. If you're still concerned, you should engage a polygrapher of your own choosing for a second opinion."

"Maybe I will."

"Do you want to go over any of the questions in advance, or rehearse before we start?"

"No, they're what I expected. Let's get on with it."

Fields stood and grabbed a pair of rubber tubes. "If you'll unbutton your shirt, I'll attach these pneumos—sorry, that's jargon for pneumograph tubes—to your chest and abdomen. They're actually tiny, specially designed bellows that detect changes in respiration rate and involuntary muscle movement."

When they were hooked up, he slipped two metal fingerplates over the tips of Keele's left ring and index fingers.

"These GSRs connect to a galvanograph that measures galvanic skin response and changes in resistance to electrical currents caused by increased sweat-gland activity."

Keefe fidgeted and watched quietly.

"Are you all right?" Fields asked.

"I'm okay."

"Last is the blood pressure cuff like the one your doctor uses when he gives you a physical." He wrapped it around Keefe's right biceps and tightened the Velcro, then plugged the wires into the cardiosphygmograph to record blood pressure and pulse rate.

"That's it," Fields said. "Ready?"

"Get on with it."

"I'll read each question slowly, exactly as they appear on your copy. After each of your answers, I'll wait ten seconds before asking the next question. Remember, sit still, breathe normally, and answer all questions only 'yes' or 'no.' "

Fields picked up a pencil. "Is your name Reginald Keefe?"

"You know it is."

"Yes or no, Judge."

"Yes."

Four graph lines scrolled across the screen and Fields checked off question 1.

"Are you fifty-two years old?"

"Yes."

Fields watched the graphs, and checked off question 2.

"Are you employed as the presiding Santa Rita County Superior Court Judge of the criminal courts?"

"Yes."

"Have you been a judge for more than ten years?"

"Yes."

"Have you practiced, prepared, or been coached in techniques that might enable you to defeat the purpose of this test?"

"No."

"Were you acquainted with Judge Jemima Tucker?"

"Yes."

Fields studied the graphs, made a note on the paper, and checked off question 6.

"At any time, did you engage in sexual intercourse with Jemima Tucker?"

"Yes."

"Did you engage in sexual intercourse with Jemima Tucker on Friday, January eleventh, of this year?"

"Yes."

Fields studied the graphs, scribbled another note, and checked off question 8.

"Did you kill Jemima Tucker?"

"No."

"Do you know who killed Jemima Tucker?"

"No."

"Do you know why Jemima Tucker was killed?"

"No."

Fields scrutinized the graph lines after each of the last three questions and answers, but made no notes before placing check marks beside questions 9, 10, and 11.

"Thank you. Now, I'll ask each of the questions a second time. Are you ready?"

"Yes."

Fields repeated, and Keefe answered, each of the eleven questions three times while Fields ran three complete sets of graphs. Then he removed his test equipment from Keefe's body, shut down the laptop, and stowed the polygraph machine in an aluminum attaché case.

"Thanks again, Judge," Fields said. "I'll write up my report immediately, and have a copy to you within twenty-four hours."

"Do you need me to explain any of my responses to the questions?"

"No."

"Did I pass?"

"I'm required to state my findings in writing to McCaskill, with a copy to you."

Keefe stood and buttoned his shirt. "We've known each other for years, Inspector. Haven't I always treated you with respect in my court?"

"Yes."

"Then, show me the same respect. I was in love with Jemima Tucker. I had sex with her the night she was murdered, yes, but I didn't kill her. Your test couldn't have indicated that I had anything to do with her death, because I didn't."

Fields looked at Keefe for several seconds. "My report will state that the test unequivocally indicates that you answered every question completely and truthfully, and that based on that test, it is my opinion that you neither killed Judge Jemima Tucker nor have any knowledge concerning the circumstances of her death."

CHAPTER

31

"You HAD NO BUSINESS giving Keefe a polygraph last night before clearing it with me."

"I didn't need your permission. Besides, your investigation was stalled. I figured it could use a jump start."

"You figured wrong."

"Your investigation turned up zilch in almost three weeks."

"You run the DA's office, McCaskill. I'll run my investigation."

"Starting when? Some looney whacks out a Superior Court Judge, then you and Mackay waste three weeks hassling Sanchez and Keefe, not to mention trotting off to Spain, diddling each other at tax-payers' expense."

Granz leaned forward in his chair and pointed his finger. "Watch your mouth. I won't take any shit off you."

"You're the one who'd better watch himself. Point your finger at me again, I'll bust you for threatening a prosecutor."

"You talk big."

"If you can't handle the Tucker investigation, say so and I'll call the Attorney General in to handle it for you."

"Stay out of my business, McCaskill."

McCaskill slid his chair closer to his desk, leaned forward with his elbows on the desktop, interlaced his fingers, and rested his chin on his hands. "Like you stayed out of mine?"

"What're you talking about?"

"You stuck your nose in my business when you let Mackay out of jail last night."

"She bailed."

"You posted bail for her."

"Same thing, she's my—" He caught himself in time. "Just stay outta my face."

"Look, Granz, she's your girlfriend, everyone knows that. But don't get carried away, I'm telling you how it looks to outsiders."

"I don't give a shit how it looks."

Granz walked to the door, then turned with his hand on the knob. "You must've stuck your nose halfway up Keefe's ass to get him to sign a warrant for her arrest on that flimsy evidence."

"Flimsy my foot. Think with your brain instead of your dick for a change. Did the tooth fairy board that plane at thirty-five thousand feet, slip Simmons a dose of digitalis, then fly off without anybody noticing?"

Granz shrugged but didn't answer.

"Don't let Mackay take you down with her. That bitch murdered Simmons and I'm going to prove it, even if she did wiggle her cute ass at you and swear she's innocent."

"I can take care of myself. And don't ever talk about her like that again, or I'll personally see that you're the one who goes down. Permanently."

"That's twice you threatened me. I won't let it slide a third time."

"Fuck off."

"Keep your nose out of the Mackay prosecution, or I'll let the press know you posted her bail. If the reporters don't run you out of office, I'll do it myself."

CHAPTER

32

"What's that?" She was naked.

He peered through narrow slits in the hood of his black robe, strapped Kathryn Mackay to the table, tapped the syringe, and shot a stream of liquid at the light dangling from a frayed wire. It vaporized when it hit the hot bulb.

"Sodium thiopental, pancuronium bromide, and potassium chloride."

"Will it hurt?"

"No worse than a blood test." His hands were rough and had dirt under the fingernails. "You've had that done?"

"Sure, but the doctors washed their hands."

"It doesn't matter if murderers get infections."

"I'm innocent."

"They all say that."

The needle slid in and the executioner injected venom into her vein. He pulled the needle out and tossed it into the trash can.

"How long does it take?" Kathryn asked.

"When you hear the bell, you'll be dead."

When the bell rang, Kathryn jumped up, knocking her half-empty coffee cup off the nightstand. The doorbell rang again.

After Emma left for school, Kathryn had brewed coffee, climbed back into bed, and fallen asleep. At noon, she made more coffee and thought about calling a lawyer to get started on her defense against the murder charge, but decided to turn on the afternoon soaps instead. She fell asleep again as Rosie O'Donnell was introducing that afternoon's guests.

The doorbell rang a third time. Emma's yellow Lab, Sam, trotted to the front door, sniffed, ran back to the bedroom, laid his head on the edge of Kathryn's bed, and whined. She rolled over and Sam licked her.

She wiped her face with the sheet. "Go away, you've got bad breath."

The dog tucked his tail between his legs and sat. She tossed the blanket off and swung her legs over the side of the bed, then inspected herself in her dresser mirror. "Jesus, I look like a bag lady."

When the doorbell rang a fourth time, she tightened the belt on her terry robe. "All right, all right, I'm coming."

Sam dashed to the door and wagged his tail. Kathryn patted him. He drooled on the tile floor.

"Some watchdog you are. You'd be glad to see Jack the Ripper if he came to visit."

When she opened the door, Sam stuck his wet nose on Jim Fields' hand.

He stroked the dog's muzzle. "Hi ya, pal, I'm glad to see you, too." Then he made eye contact with his ex-boss. "May I come in?"

"Sure."

She led him to the living room, sat on the sofa and tucked her legs up under her.

Fields dropped onto the edge of a matching chair, unconsciously smoothed the empty sleeve of his suit coat, and stared at her across the coffee table. " 'Scuse my French, but you look like shit."

"Try being charged with murder—see how *you* look." She combed her thick hair with her fingers. "It could be worse. I suppose I could be in jail."

He handed her a folded legal document. "I'm really sorry, Kathryn, but that's why I'm here. That's a bench warrant."

She examined it and dropped it onto the sofa. "Murder with special circumstances?"

"McCaskill was waiting at Keefe's chambers at eight o'clock this morning to file an amended indictment."

"On what grounds?"

"Murder by poisoning."

"Digitalis isn't a poison."

"McCaskill's position is that when it's intentionally administered in a lethal dose, it's a poison."

"This elevates it to a death-penalty case, and automatically revokes my bail."

"I know."

She grabbed the phone. "If that bastard sent you here to take me to jail again, I need to call Emma's school."

"He ordered me to not let you use the phone before we get to jail, but I guess I'll take my chances when it comes to Emma. Go ahead."

She dropped the handset back into the cradle. "No, I'll get dressed."

"He ordered me to not take my eyes off you until you're booked, to make sure you don't stash a weapon or try to kill yourself."

Kathryn didn't answer, but got up and walked to her bedroom. She stopped beside the bed, untied her robe and dropped it to the floor, then turned around, naked.

Fields flushed. "I'll turn my back."

"Not necessary. I don't want you to lie when he asks if you followed orders. But, there's one thing you could do for me."

"Name it."

"After you book me into jail, call Ruth. Ask her to come downstairs and take Sam home with her. She has a key."

"Done. Anything else?"

"What about Emma?"

"McCaskill made it clear he'd fire me if I interfered this time. He's arranging to have CPS meet her after school."

"The son of a bitch really hates me, doesn't he?"

"Yes."

"Does Dave know about this?"

"No. McCaskill scheduled a meet with Granz in the DA's office this morning, to prevent anyone contacting him."

"Why? It's a no-bail warrant. Even Dave can't help me this time."

CHAPTER

33

NEWS OF THE DISTRICT ATTORNEY'S ARREST spread through the jail grapevine like a wildfire. When Mackay walked into the recreation room and grabbed a book, a dozen female inmates in maroon jumpsuits fell silent.

She ignored them, walked across the room, sat in a chair at the far corner, and pretended to read.

A fat Hispanic woman with holes in her nose where silver studs used to be slid a chair over. She sat down in front of Mackay and punched the book with her fist.

"Remember me, abogada puta?"

"Sylvia Gomez."

Gomez pointed to the webbing between her left thumb and forefinger, where a cross with the initials

VSC was crudely tattooed. "You know Villa San Carlos?"

"I've heard of your gang. So what?"

"We badasses."

"Sure you are."

Gomez wiggled her finger at a second woman. She was slim but buffed, pretty in a hard sort of way, with muscular arms that hung from the rolled-up sleeves of her jumpsuit. She gave Gomez a thumbs-up, then pulled a stool over and sat beside Gomez, penning Mackay in.

"You know mi amiga?" Gomez asked.

"No."

"Se llama Letitia Rios."

"That's nice."

"She do what I tell her," Gomez said.

Mackay looked at Rios. "Congratulations."

Gomez snapped her fingers. "She kill you that fast, I tell her to."

"Go away."

"Don't think so. How you like bein' in jail?"

Mackay returned her gaze to the book. It was Steinbeck's *East of Eden* in an old green hard-cover.

Gomez ripped the book from Mackay's hands. "They say you kill that gringo doctor."

"I didn't kill anybody."

Gomez laughed. "Nobody in jail did nothin'. Me neither, but you busted me anyways."

"My office was doing its job, Gomez."

"I dint do nothin' illegal."

"You're a gangbanger and a drug dealer."

"¡Vete a tomar por culo!" Gomez slapped Mackay's face.

Mackay's eyes watered, and she tried to stand up, but Gomez shoved her back.

"¡Idiota de los cojones! You hear me, bitch?" Gomez demanded. "I tol' you I dint do nothin'."

"Sure you didn't."

"Leas' I ain' no murderer."

"Not yet, anyway," Mackay said in a show of bravado she didn't feel. "Now that you've shown everybody how tough you are, get lost."

"No way."

Mackay glanced around the room, but none of the other inmates looked at her.

"Patado tu culo," Gomez told her.

"You won't kick my ass in front of a dozen witnesses."

Gomez turned and flicked her head. Everyone except Rios filed out of the room, then she turned back to Mackay.

"What witnesses?"

Mackay leaned forward. "I'm leaving."

Before she could get to her feet, Gomez's fist slammed into her face, shattering bone and tearing cartilage. Her brain told her to get up, but her body refused.

Gomez slammed her fist into Mackay's left eye, and a third blow smashed into the side of her head.

"You wan' some more, bitch?" Gomez asked.

"Go to hell."

Gomez' fist crashed into Mackay's mouth. A tooth dropped into the pool of blood in her lap, hot pain shot through her head, and the ringing in her ears shouted, *get the hell out of here before she kills you.* She couldn't see out of her swollen-shut left eye, and her lips were shredded.

"Kiss my ass."

"You think you some tough cunt? We see 'bout that."

Rios pulled out a shank, a spoon that had been flattened and ground to a razor edge, its handle wrapped with medical tape. She slashed the front of Mackay's jumpsuit and yanked it open. "Pretty small tits, I think I cut 'em both off."

Rios sliced a crude cross deep into the skin between Mackay's breasts, then carved *VSC* into the skin of her abdomen. "Give you a souvenir."

Gomez leaned forward, her face inches from Mackay's. "You wan' her to cut your heart out? You wanna die?"

Mackay willed herself not to cry. "No."

"Beg."

"No."

"Then we kill you right now."

Mackay screwed up her courage for one last bluff. "Stop now, and no one'll know who did this, otherwise you'll be arrested within a hour, and my prosecutors'll see you get the death penalty. You'll die slower than me."

"You talk brave."

"What's it going to be, Gomez?"

"I thinkin'."

"If you're going to kill me, do it."

Gomez looked at Rios, shook her head, then stood.

"I let you off this time, gringa. Next time I kill you myself."

"I know the jailhouse drill, now get out of here."

After they left, Mackay tried to push herself out of the chair, but collapsed to the floor.

The last thing she remembered was lying on her back looking at the ceiling, wondering if Emma had aced her math exam that morning.

CHAPTER
34

"EMMA, MAY I SPEAK with you, please?"

Ashley leaned close and whispered, "Uh-oh! What'd you do?"

"Nothing."

"You must have or she'd have sent her assistant to get you."

Margaret Cheng, principal of Holy Cross Middle School, picked her way through the whooping, hollering students who spilled out of their last classes for the day. "Please excuse us, Ashley."

Ashley hugged Emma. "See you at choir."

"Emma will be excused from choir practice today," Cheng said. "Now run along so you aren't late."

Emma turned to the school principal. "Am I in big trouble?"

Cheng put her arm around Emma's shoulder. "Would you come with me, please?"

Emma followed Cheng into The Office, where students never went unless they had done something wrong. When Cheng swung open the door to her private office, a woman was waiting.

Emma looked at Cheng. "What's going on?"

"Mrs. Guererro wants to speak to you, Emma."

Short and heavyset with dark olive skin and piercing brown eyes, Frederika Guererro's grandmotherly demeanor around children belied her tenacious intensity, qualities that were essential to the head of the County Human Resources Agency's Child Protective Services Division.

"I've worked with your mother, and heard a lot about you, Emma. I'm happy to finally meet you."

"Thank you."

Guererro glanced at Cheng. "Would you excuse us?"

When the door closed, Guererro said softly, "I have some bad news."

Emma's eyes widened as she remembered the day she heard her father had been shot to death in a Los Angeles courtroom. "Is my mom dead?"

"No."

"Did something happen to her?"

"Yes."

"What?"

"She's been beaten up."

"Take me to see her."

"I wish I could, but it's not that simple. She is in custody. Do you know what that means?"

"She didn't do it."

"If you'll tell me what you've heard, I'll try to help you sort things out."

Emma glanced around like she might take off, but perched nervously on the edge of the chair. "Some kids said my mom got arrested and fired from her job because she murdered Doctor Simmons."

"Did you believe them?"

"No."

"Well, it's not true that your mother got fired. She's still District Attorney, but she's taking some time off."

"Did she get arrested like they said?"

"I'm afraid so."

"My mom wouldn't kill anyone."

"I don't think so, either, so if Mr. McCaskill made a mistake, they'll figure it out."

"Who beat her up?"

"Some inmates at the jail. Officers called an ambulance, and they took her to the hospital."

"Can I see her?"

"Not right now."

"You didn't come to tell me about Mom, did you?"

"Sometimes children are left alone temporarily, with no family to take care of them. It's my job to help."

"I'm not a child, I'm twelve."

"I understand, but the law requires—"

"I won't go with you."

"You have no choice, Emma."

"I can stay at my friend Ashley's house, it'll be all right with her mom and dad, they like me."

"I'm sure they do, but—"

"Then call Sheriff Granz, you know him, I can stay at his house."

"Emma . . ."

Emma jumped up. "You can't make me, damn you!"

"You have to go with me. It'll be better for us both if you don't make me force you."

"I don't care what's better for you, I hate you."

"I know this isn't easy for you."

"How would you know? Did anyone ever come to your school and lock you up?"

"I'm not going to lock you up."

"Same thing. If you really wanted to help me, you'd take me to Dave's house."

"I can't, I'm sorry."

"You're a liar. You aren't sorry."

CHAPTER

35

EMMA STOOD JUST INSIDE the door to Kathryn's hospital room and stared in horror, barely able to choke the words out between sobs. "Why did those women beat you up, Mom?"

"They thought I was someone else, honey, someone they don't like." Kathryn patted the mattress.

Emma sat on the side of the bed and gently stroked her mother's bruised, swollen face. "Does it hurt?"

"Not as bad as it looks."

"You didn't kill Doctor Simmons, right?"

"Of course not."

"Then why does Mr. McCaskill think you did?"

"I don't know."

"I hate him!"

"Em . . ."

"I hate Mrs. Guererro, too."

Kathryn glanced at Dave. "Frederika Guererro, from Child Protective Services?"

"She put Emma in foster care for the night," Dave explained.

"Mrs. Roseboro's," Emma said. "I told Mrs. Guererro I wanted to stay with Dave, but she wouldn't take me there. I got mad and said 'damn you.' That wasn't very Christian, was it?"

"No, but under the circumstances God will forgive you." Kathryn tried to prop herself up, but groaned and lay back down. "Dammit, Dave, why didn't you go get Emma from the foster home when you found out?"

"McCaskill timed your arrest so that by the time I got the word, CPS offices had closed for the day. I called Guererro at home, but she wouldn't tell me where they'd placed Emma without a court order."

"Did you tell her . . ."

"No, she assured me Emma was safe."

"No thanks to that SOB McCaskill. Well, at least you were able to pick Em up at school this afternoon and bring her to see me."

"I didn't pick her up."

"How did she get here?"

"I didn't go to school today," Emma said. "When Mrs. Roseboro dropped me off at school this morning, I ran away."

"You what!"

"She came to my office just as I was leaving for the hospital," Dave said.

"Oh, Emma!" Kathryn sighed through her swollen lips. "Where did you go?"

"The mall."

"Today's Thursday—didn't anyone ask why you weren't at school?"

"There's always kids in the food court."

"How did you get to Dave's office?"

"Walked." She paused, then brightened. "I'm glad you and Dave got married, now I can stay with him."

"Dave? You told her?"

"On the way here. I couldn't let her worry about having a home. Didn't figure you'd mind under the circumstances."

"Dave and I wanted to tell you together, Em, to make it a really special occasion. But when—well, then we didn't know how."

"That's okay."

Kathryn held Emma's hand. "Were you happy when Dave told you?"

"Sure."

"Surprised?"

"Oh, Mom, course not, it was inevitable."

Kathryn laughed despite her shredded lips. "I suppose it was."

"Dependency hearing's scheduled for tomorrow, Babe," Dave said. "The court'll appoint lawyers for you and Emma. I'll set up a meet with them in the morning before the hearing, show 'em the marriage certificate, tell you won't contest the dependency hearing if they place Emma with me."

Kathryn's swollen, blackened eyes filled with tears.

Dave looked at Emma, then at Kathryn. "Did I say something wrong?"

She dabbed at her tender eyes with a tissue. "Men don't understand the first thing about a woman's emotions."

"Mom, will you have to go back to jail when you get out of the hospital?"

"Yes, until I prove I'm innocent."

"How can you do that?"

"I talked to some lawyers this afternoon. By tonight, I'll have hired one of them to work with me to prove my innocence."

Dave sat on the bed beside Emma, dug in his pants pocket, and fished out a handful of change, which he handed to her. "I'm thirsty, Em. Would you please find a soda machine and buy three Diet Cokes."

Emma juggled the coins. "There must be five bucks here. Can I buy a Snickers?"

"You'll spoil your dinner."

"You sound just like Mom. C'mon, I'm starving."

"Okay."

When Emma left, Kathryn smiled and picked up Dave's hand. "Well, she was really impressed about us getting married. Inevitable, indeed!"

"At twelve years old, things are a lot simpler. She probably saw it coming all along, even when you and I didn't. Makes you wonder about the old adage that age brings wisdom, huh?"

"I'll say."

"What lawyers did you call?"

"I didn't, I was just trying to reassure Emma. I wanted to talk to you about it because I really don't know who to call."

"Start with *what* you need, that'll tell you *who*. You

need a lawyer who's got the guts to do battle, fight a long, bloody, no-holds-barred war, do whatever it takes to win."

"You make it sound like the lawyer would be more important than the case, even for someone who's innocent."

"You're the best prosecutor I know, Babe, but right now you're sounding like a typical defendant. If you were thinking straight, you'd know that criminal defense is about persuasion. The right lawyer's impact on a jury can make the difference between acquittal and life in prison. Think about Johnnie Cochran and O.J. You need a bulldog with an overpowering personality, yet enough charisma to sway a jury despite the evidence."

"*Despite* the evidence! McCaskill doesn't have a witness who saw me dump digitalis in Simmons' Diet Coke—does he?"

"The important thing is that your lawyer is totally dedicated to your welfare. McCaskill's a prick, but he's a damn good prosecutor, and there's plenty of evidence for a lawyer to overcome."

"You didn't answer." She stared at him for several seconds, but decided not to press. "Anyway, his evidence is all circumstantial."

"We both know that more often than not there's no witness to a murder. Besides, eyewitnesses are less reliable than solid circumstantial evidence. And his evidence looks pretty damn solid to me."

"Do I have a chance?"

"Only if your lawyer's creative, resourceful, tough as nails, and a kick-ass cross-examiner. Someone who, if McCaskill opens up the tiniest crack, will drive a Mack truck through it."

"Any suggestions?"

"What about James Brosnahan of San Francisco?"

"His representation of die-hard bin Ladin supporter John Walker provoked such an uproar at his firm and with his clients, I wouldn't want him by my side."

"You can't ignore the fact that your case is politically charged. McCaskill's going to drag you through the dirt, make you look like a monster. He knows enough about you, Simmons, and me that he might pull it off, too. What he lacks in facts he'll make up. You need a lawyer who can bring out your best so the jury's sympathetic."

"Someone local who jurors know and respect and who's tried enough cases against McCaskill to know all his sleazy tactics and can head them off beforehand."

"Roger Griffith."

"He was the first person I thought of, too. He's the best defense attorney in the county. I'll call him as soon as you and Emma take off."

"You need rest. Get some sleep, call him tomorrow morning."

"There's no time to waste. I'm going to refuse to waive time, make McCaskill take me to trial right away."

"What if Griffith doesn't agree?"

"I'll hire someone else."

"That'd get you to trial right away and make it harder for McCaskill to prepare his case, but it might backfire. Griffith needs time to find ways to punch holes in McCaskill's case. I'm not sure refusing to waive time's a good idea."

"Me neither, but if I don't, I won't get to trial for a year or longer. I won't live that long in jail."

"I'll put you in 'Q.' " He referred to the secure section of the jail where high-risk and extremely violent inmates were housed to segregate them from the general population, and isolate them from each other.

"Even in Q you can't protect me that long. Someone'll eventually figure a way to get to me, and next time, they'll kill me."

"You're probably right."

"I *am* right. And I need to end this for Emma's sake."

Dave sighed. "I know. Let's hope if Griffith agrees to defend you that he can put together a strong defense quickly."

"If he can't, no one can. Now, go find Em so I can say good night, then get out of here so I can phone Griffith."

CHAPTER
36

THE OLD RUSTY ECONOLINE VAN creaked into the parking place beside Granz' Buick.

The driver shut off the engine, and cracked the driver's window to keep the windows from fogging up. He sat listening to KESP, a Spanish music station, until 8:45 A.M., then pressed the fake gray mustache against his upper lip to set the glue, pushed the phony bifocals onto his nose, placed a gray human-hair wig on his head, and secured it with a wide-brimmed straw hat, then checked himself in the mirror.

"Muy bueno—un bracero anciano."

He pocketed the car keys and dashed toward the court building, the size-thirteen Goodwill work boots rubbing blisters on the heels of his size-nine feet, the tattered, dirty shirt and jacket doing little to protect him from the cold, penetrating morning drizzle.

The metal detector didn't pick up the cheap Polaroid inside his jacket because it was mostly plastic. He shuffled over to the calendar posted outside the door to Judge Jesse A. Woods' Superior Court Six.

A deputy spotted him trying to figure it out, and strolled over. "Need some help, old man?"

"Sí. ¿Habla Español?"

"No, and I figured you prob'ly couldn't read English, either. Whatcha lookin' for?"

He pointed at the line that said, Dependency hearing, *in re Emma Mackay.* "What that say—traffic court?"

"No, that's juvenile court."

"Oh. I get speeding ticket, got to see the judge."

The deputy pointed. "That way, round the corner, downstairs, to your left."

"Gracias."

"You're welcome. Have a nice day."

He watched the deputy return to his station, say something to the other cop, and point his way. They both laughed, then turned their attention back to the metal detector.

"Racist pig, I speak better English than you," *he muttered. He made sure no one was watching, pulled out a cheap Polaroid without a flash unit, and surreptitiously snapped several quick shots of Emma Mackay, who was standing by a large potted plant across the hall from the courtroom door.*

When he spotted Granz leave the bathroom and head Emma's way, he pocketed the snapshots, dropped the camera in a trash can, and headed toward traffic court.

In the basement cafeteria, he grabbed a cup of coffee and a bran muffin, then ran back to the van. He stuck the key in the ignition, started the engine, and turned the heater up high. Then he removed the straw hat, wig, glasses, and mustache, and tossed them on the pavement next to Granz' car.

Sipping his coffee and nibbling at the muffin, he flipped through the photos and studied the face.

"Perfect. I'd remember that face anywhere," he finally said aloud. "These will do just fine."

CHAPTER

37

THE DOOR ON THE RIGHT SIDE of the wall behind the vacant jury box in Superior Court Six swung open.

Bailiff Harold Benjamin stood. "All rise. Department Twelve of the Santa Rita County Superior Court is now in session, the Honorable Jesse Augustus Woods presiding."

Santa Rita County had only ten courts and judges, but Department Twelve was a special designation for the separate court established by California law in every county to meet the unique needs of juveniles—persons under eighteen years of age.

Woods swept past the jury box, settled into the chair behind the bench, slipped on drugstore reading glasses, and gazed into the almost-empty room.

"Please be seated."

In his sixties, Woods was tall and athletic, with square shoulders, large hands, and a thick mop of unruly white hair that defied both time and comb. His stern, bearded, intense face and booming voice belied a well-known underlying sensitivity.

A respected jurist with a deep affinity for kids, Woods had presided over juvenile court for many years. During testimony he often appeared bored, turning aside and gazing into space or closing his eyes, but lawyers who practiced before him knew that this was simply a technique for concentrating—he missed nothing.

Court Clerk Cathy Radina announced, "In the Superior Court of the State of California, in and for the County of Santa Rita, case number DP12-200237, adjudication hearing for dependency petition of minor child Emma S. Mackay, the People . . ."

Woods noted Emma's worried look, and removed his half-glasses. "Let's skip the formalities. For the record, the Court notes the presence of Frederika Guererro of Child Protective Services and their attorney, County Counsel Daniel Burford, Court-appointed attorney Martin Belker for Emma Mackay, and Roger Griffith representing Kathryn Mackay and Sheriff David Granz."

He paused to let the court reporter catch up. "Bring in Kathryn Mackay."

Benjamin opened the door through which Judge Woods had previously entered, disappeared for a couple of minutes, then returned holding Kathryn Mackay by the right elbow. A collective gasp rose from the room.

She looked like she'd gone fifteen rounds with the heavyweight champ. And lost. A bandage was wrapped around her left ear and forehead, and her face had ballooned to twice its normal size, reducing her eyes to tiny dark slits. Her whole face was a massive purple bruise, and by pulling the gauze from her nostrils, she released two trickles of bloody mucus onto her puffy lips.

Dwarfed by the oversized maroon jail jumpsuit, she duckwalked down the row of jury seats and sat in chair 6, then tried to smile. She raised her hands to wipe her mouth, but the handcuff chain, which was looped through a heavy belt and connected to ankle shackles, stopped them at midchest. Benjamin wiped the mess from her mouth.

Emma stared for a moment, pushed her chair away from the table, and headed toward Kathryn. Benjamin stepped in front to intercept her.

Woods cut him off. "Let her be with her mother for a moment, please. Step back and give them some room, and remove the restraints."

When Benjamin unlocked the handcuffs and shackles, Emma dropped into a chair beside her mother. "The Judge will let me live with Dave, won't he, Mom?"

"I hope so, honey, but it's his decision."

"I don't want to go back to Mrs. Roseboro's tonight."

"I know."

"How long will it take Judge Woods to make up his mind?"

"We'll know before we leave. Now, please go sit

with Dave and Mr. Griffith so we can get this over with, okay?"

Woods watched until Emma sat down, established eye contact with her, and winked. "This morning, Mr. Griffith submitted to the Court a certificate establishing that Kathryn Mackay and David Granz are now husband and wife."

He looked at Burford. "Did you get a copy?"

Burford rose. "Yes. As a result, I request a continuance until next week."

"What for?"

"To ascertain the legal status of the so-called marriage between Ms. Mackay and Sheriff Granz."

"What makes you doubt its legitimacy?"

"It was performed in a foreign country, and—"

"Sit down, Mr. Burford. Last I heard, Spain was a civilized nation. If I think your concerns ought to play a part in my decision, I'll hear them later."

"The marriage certificate could be a phony."

"So could your law degree. Court is in recess while I speak with Emma in chambers."

Woods walked to counsel table and leaned over so that his eyes were at Emma's level. "Would you mind coming to my chambers so we could talk privately?"

She looked at Dave, who nodded.

"I don't mind."

Woods pulled his robe over his head, hung it on a hook behind the door, loosened his tie, and suggested they sit on his leather sofa.

"You know why we're here today, right, Emma?"

"Why don't you let my mom go home so I can

stay with her? She told me she didn't kill Doctor Simmons."

"It's not that simple, Em—may I call you Em?"

"That's what Dave and my mom call me."

"Okay, you call me Jesse."

He leaned back and crossed his legs. "Em, I don't give a hoot what those lawyers out there say, the only thing I care about is that you're safe and happy, that you have a good home, and that you go to school every day. Do you understand?"

"Yes."

"Mrs. Guererro says you skipped school yesterday. What happened?"

"She forced me to go to Mrs. Roseboro's. I don't like her."

"You don't even know her. I'm being straight with you, why don't you be straight with me, too."

"I was scared. I wanted to see my mom and Dave. If you send me back, I'll keep running away."

"You could get in a lot of trouble."

"I don't care."

Woods looked at her for a long time, and she held his gaze.

"What do you suggest?" he finally asked.

"I want to stay with Dave. He's almost my dad now."

Woods contemplated. "If I let you stay with him, will you promise you won't run away again, and that you'll go to school every day?"

"Yes, I promise."

Woods pulled a business card from his wallet, scribbled something on the back, and handed it to Emma.

"This is my private telephone number. Call me every Friday afternoon at five o'clock—no exceptions—and tell me how things are going."

"Okay." She slipped the card into her wallet. "Does this mean I can stay with Dave until my mom proves she's innocent and gets out of jail?"

"That's what it means."

Emma put her arms around his neck. "Thank you, Jesse."

When she let go, he lifted his judicial robe off the hook and slipped it over his head, then extended his hand and helped her to her feet.

"Then why don't you and I go back out there and tell everyone what we decided."

CHAPTER

38

THE SATURDAY MORNING, March 23, *Santa Rita Centennial* lead story began:

EX-DA FIGHT AGAINST DEATH STARTS MONDAY

The jury trial in the highly publicized murder case of ex-DA Kathryn Mackay begins at 9 A.M. next Monday. Renowned local defense attorney Roger Griffith will make a last-ditch effort to throw out the special circumstance of murder by poison to save Mackay from the death penalty. Jury selection is scheduled to start Tuesday morning. Judge Reginald

Keefe has ordered most of the courtroom
spectator section reserved for the media,
with the few remaining seats raffled off
to the public.

By dusk the next day, the media and public
swarmed over the County Government Center like
yellow jackets at a Fourth of July picnic. Trucks, RVs,
and tents jostled for space in the parking lot with television broadcast vans, which pointed their antennae
at invisible geostationary satellites that collected,
then scattered their pictures and commentary instan-
taneously across the state.

By nightfall, the acrid odor of cooking meat and
charcoal lighter permeated the cool spring air, and
mingled with the gasoline-oil fumes from portable
generators that struggled to power dozens of news
anchors' dressing rooms, scores of light banks, and
hundreds of coffeepots. An impromptu band blasted
out country and western music below a makeshift
bandstand until the Sheriff's Department shut them
down at 2:00 A.M.

Shortly after, lines started to form on the courthouse steps.

CHAPTER

39

DISTRICT ATTORNEY NEAL MCCASKILL sat by himself, yellow legal pads and a stack of transcripts, briefs, and police reports on the prosecution table. He didn't look up when Bailiff Patti O'Connor helped Kathryn Mackay limp to the defense table.

Mackay had no makeup on and had trimmed her hair very short, concessions to the austere Blaine Street facilities. She wore a steel-gray Gianni pants suit with a white silk open-necked blouse and charcoal-gray low-heel shoes.

"Kathryn, what happened, why are you limping?" Roger Griffith stood while she seated herself.

She tapped her knee with a fingertip. "There's a plastic brace on my knee to prevent me from running—as if I'd try. But I have to wear pants instead of a skirt so the jury can't see it."

"I was afraid you'd been attacked again."

"Don't worry about me. A detention officer escorts me to meals, to the shower—anyplace outside Q. I'm as safe as possible under the circumstances."

"I hope so."

In his late forties, Griffith stood more than six feet tall, but his stooped posture made him look shorter. With mousy brown hair and an aquiline nose, he was rather ordinary-looking, but his intense blue eyes darted about, continually scrutinizing and evaluating every aspect of his surroundings. In his charcoal business suit, gray shirt, black necktie, and black wingtips, he looked more like a corporate attorney than a criminal defense lawyer.

O'Connor admitted the media and spectators at 8:45. At exactly 9:00 A.M., Monday, March 25, Judge Reginald Keefe acknowledged the District Attorney and the defense counsel, and convened court.

"The defendant has brought a PC 995 motion attacking the sufficiency of evidence in support of a charge of murder with special circumstances, and seeking to reinstate the defendant to bail."

He turned to the defense table. "It's your motion, Mr. Griffith. Let's hear what you have to say."

"The defense has a witness to call, Judge."

McCaskill objected. "Defense counsel knows if any evidence supports an indictment, the Court can't dismiss it, and the prosecution has already satisfied the Court as to the sufficiency of the evidence that supports the charge."

Keefe turned to the defense table. "I'm inclined to agree, Counselor."

Griffith shook his head. "The Court isn't precluded from receiving information outside the record, Judge, and the defendant has a right to call its own witness."

"What witness?"

"Doctor Morgan Nelson."

McCaskill's face turned red. "I demand an offer of proof that Nelson might impeach his own scientific findings, reports, conclusions, his statements to investigators, or that his testimony today might negate an element of the crime charged."

"What about that, Mr. Griffith?"

"Nelson's findings and conclusions were selectively presented to the Grand Jury that led to the special-circumstance charge. Had his conclusions been fully disclosed, they would have negated a required element of the special circumstances."

Keefe sighed and flipped his hand. "Oh, all right, call your witness, but keep it brief."

"The defense calls Doctor Morgan Nelson."

Nelson raised his right hand, swore to tell the truth, and settled comfortably into the chair.

"Please state your name, Doctor, and spell your last name for the court reporter," Griffith said.

"Morgan Nelson—N-E-L-S-O-N."

"What is your occupation?"

"De facto Santa Rita County Coroner."

"Describe your education, training, and experience that qualify you to be coroner."

Keefe held his hand up in a stop signal. "Save it for trial, the Court is aware of Doctor Nelson's expertise.

The prosecution will stipulate for purposes of this hearing that Doctor Nelson is a medical expert, isn't that right, Mr. McCaskill?"

"Yes."

"Move on, Mr. Griffith."

"On January sixteenth, did you autopsy the body of Robert Simmons?"

"I did."

"Did you subsequently prepare a report as to the cause of death of Doctor Simmons, and did you later discuss that report with Mr. McCaskill?"

"Yes."

"What did your report state caused Doctor Simmons' death?"

"A digitalis overdose."

"Is digitalis a prescription medicine?"

"It is."

"But administered in massive doses, it can be fatal?"

"Yes."

"Is that true of other prescription medicines?"

"Yes, and most nonprescription medicines as well, such as aspirin."

"What about items that are neither prescribed nor over-the-counter medications."

"Such as?"

"Chocolate."

"In massive enough quantities, just about anything can be fatal, including chocolate. And salt. Even water."

"Then they're poisons?"

"Not in my opinion."

"Would it be accurate to say that if I died because I ate too much chocolate given to me by my wife, I died from the intentional administration of a poison, and my wife's a murderer?"

"That would be quite a stretch."

"You're aware that Mr. McCaskill has charged that my client killed Robert Simmons with poison, and if the jury finds this to be true, they can kill her by lethal injection?"

"Yes."

"Assuming the allegation of murder to be true for purposes of your testimony here today, is it your opinion that when Ms. Mackay administered digitalis to Robert Simmons, she administered a poison?"

"Definitely not."

"Thank you." Griffith walked back to the defense table. "No further questions."

McCaskill approached the witness stand and handed Nelson a blue brochure. "You've heard of the American Association of Poison Control Centers?"

"Of course."

"Please read the part that's highlighted in yellow, under the heading, 'What Is a Poison.' "

Nelson slipped on a pair of reading glasses. " 'A poison is any substance someone eats, breathes, gets in the eyes, or on the skin that can cause sickness or death if it gets into or on the body.' "

"Now read the single, orange-highlighted word beside the first bullet, under the caption, 'Most Dangerous Poisons.' "

" 'Medicines.' "

"Would you agree, based on that document, that the American Association of Poison Control Centers considers digitalis a deadly poison, and would not consider it 'quite a *stretch*' to find that one who intentionally overdosed another with digitalis committed murder by poison?"

"You'd have to ask them."

"I don't think that'll be necessary, Doctor, your answer is quite adequate." McCaskill retrieved the pamphlet and handed it to the court clerk to be marked as People's Exhibit 1.

"No further questions."

Keefe turned to the defense table. "Unless you have further questions for this witness, Mr. Griffith, I'm prepared to rule on your motion."

"Your Honor, I would like to be heard first."

"All right, but be brief."

Griffith touched Mackay on the shoulder, then stood and walked to the podium facing the bench.

"Murder by poisoning supports a special-circumstance murder indictment only if it is *reasonably* supported by the evidence. Mr. McCaskill distorted Doctor Nelson's findings and conclusions, and chose not to elicit his opinion about whether or not digitalis is a poison because had he done so, he would have received the answer Doctor Nelson gave today—that digitalis is *not* a poison.

"Mr. McCaskill presented selective and incomplete information to the Court in support of his amended indictment charging special circumstances. This Court must question whether the prosecution's outrageous interpretation of 'murder by poison' meets both the legal requirements and the spirit of California's death-penalty law.

"The People don't want my client to die, Your Honor, only Mr. McCaskill wants that. And he wants the State to do his killing for him. Don't let him get away with it."

Keefe contemplated. "The Court notes that the standards employed in deciding a 995 motion are highly favorable to the People—every legitimate inference that may be drawn from the evidence must be drawn in favor of the indictment, which cannot be set aside if there is rational ground for assuming an offense has been committed, and that the accused is guilty of committing it. Defense motion is denied. Step back."

Griffith returned to the defense table, but refused to sit. "In that case, Your Honor, I have another motion to make before jury selection begins," Griffith continued.

"The defense hasn't served me with a second motion," McCaskill protested.

"Mr. Griffith, you have a reputation with my colleagues for springing motions on the Court and prosecution. I won't tolerate that behavior in my court," Keefe admonished.

"I can present my motion without taking up too much of the Court's time."

Keefe motioned O'Connor to return to her station. "Oh, very well, proceed."

"Pursuant to PC 1424 and CCP 170.5, the defense moves to recuse the District Attorney and disqualify Your Honor from presiding over this trial, on the basis—"

"Objection!" McCaskill rose, shaking his head in

disgust. "For starters, a motion to recuse me must be served on my office and the Attorney General ten days in advance of a hearing. The defense has failed to meet the statute's notice requirements."

Keefe glared. "I warned you that I wouldn't tolerate any shenanigans, Mr. Griffith. How do you explain your failure to serve the DA and the Attorney General?"

"The need for this motion wasn't fully apparent until the Court's adverse ruling on my 995 motion."

A murmur arose from the spectator section of the courtroom, and Keefe slammed his gavel on the bench. "Silence! Approach the bench, Griffith! You, too, McCaskill!"

Griffith didn't move. "I request that my client be at sidebar."

"Not a chance."

"My client is a licensed attorney and an integral part of her own defense."

"Forget it. Get up here, and be quick about it."

Griffith patted Mackay's shoulder and approached the bench.

Keefe whispered so that the spectators and media couldn't hear. "What the hell do you think you're doing, Griffith?"

"Making sure my client gets a fair trial."

"What makes you think she won't?"

"I'll make that clear when I argue my motion."

Keefe paused for several seconds. "I'll close the hearing—then hear your motion."

"I object to excluding the media and public from a hearing on our motion," Griffith told him.

"Then I'm going to limit you to argument on recusing Mr. McCaskill."

"Judge . . ."

"That's my ruling, Mr. Griffith. Now, step back."

Griffith returned to the podium. "Mr. McCaskill is so incapable of acting impartially, and has a conflict of interest of such magnitude, that it renders it not just unlikely but impossible for my client to receive a fair trial. In fact, this trial would not have been pursued except for the malicious and discriminatory design of the prosecutor."

Keefe held his hand up, palm out. "Explain that."

"It's simple." Griffith pointed at McCaskill. "He wants Kathryn Mackay's job."

"That's ridiculous," McCaskill objected.

Keefe flashed him a dirty look. "You'll have an opportunity to respond."

"When District Attorney Benton was murdered," Griffith continued, "Neal McCaskill coveted the appointment to replace him. The Board of Supervisors appointed Kathryn Mackay, instead. She kept Mr. McCaskill as her Chief Deputy until his outrageous and insubordinate behavior left her no choice but to fire him."

"Judge!"

Keefe pointed at the prosecutor. "Sit down."

"He vowed to get Kathryn Mackay's job, whatever it took," Griffith continued. "McCaskill lost to my client by a landslide in the next election. Then, knowing he'd never beat her fair and square, when presented with the opportunity, he indicted her for the murder of Robert Simmons.

"But, McCaskill couldn't do this all by himself, he needed an accomplice to stack the deck against Ms. Mackay. An accomplice who Ms. Mackay suspected had committed a murder himself, an accomplice who has admitted to carrying on an illicit, extramarital affair with the murder victim—an accomplice none other than Judge Reginald Keefe."

"Approach the damn bench, Griffith!"

Spittle ran from the corners of Keefe's mouth and his face glowed red. "Goddammit, Griffith, one more word of this bullshit in my court, and you'll be in jail on a contempt charge faster than you can ask what the fuck happened."

Griffith returned Keefe's stare. "I have DA Chief of Investigators James Fields under subpoena. He'll testify that you admitted during a polygraph examination that you had sex with Judge Tucker the day she was murdered."

"You son of a bitch, I passed the damn poly."

"True, and polygraph results are inadmissible in court. But your admission to Inspector Fields isn't."

"I didn't murder Jemima."

"Doesn't matter. By the time Fields finishes testifying, your career will be history whether you murdered her or not."

"You know I have to deny your motion."

"I've got to consider grounds for appeal if it comes to that."

"Finish your motion. Now, step back, please."

Rather than return to the podium, Griffith walked around the defense table, resumed his seat, and rested his hand on Mackay's.

"To summarize, Your Honor, the defense contends that Mr. McCaskill used and abused the power and authority of his office for the purpose of bringing an unjustified, discriminatory, and biased prosecution against my client. For those reasons, the defense moves to recuse the District Attorney from this case."

"This Court cannot assume, on the basis of mere allegations by the defense, that the District Attorney is biased against the defendant because they previously worked together, or because Mr. McCaskill exercised his right as an American to run for public office."

Keefe removed his glasses, leaned on his elbows, and interlaced his fingers. "On the other hand, the Court acknowledges the serious nature of the issues raised in Mr. Griffith's motion, and will remain diligent to overcome any doubt that might attach to these proceedings, concerning the defendant's right to a fair and impartial trial. Defense motion to recuse the District Attorney is denied."

Griffith shot back. "I request a continuance until tomorrow morning to allow the defense time to decide whether to file a writ with the appellate court to stay this Court's ruling."

Kathryn leaned toward Griffith. "You need to start selecting a jury. We both knew I was in deep shit when Keefe assigned the case to himself. If we tried to bump him, even if we succeeded, who knows who he would have assigned in his place, better the devil we know than the devil we don't. Besides, no appellate court'll overturn Keefe's ruling."

"I just spent two hours dragging the DA through

the mud. It'll be wasted unless every potential juror in the jury pool watches it on the six-o'clock news or reads about it in tomorrow morning's newspaper."

"Very well," Keefe ruled. "Jury selection will commence at nine o'clock tomorrow morning."

CHAPTER
40

"LADIES AND GENTLEMEN, before today's session we swore you in and had you fill out a questionnaire. This questionnaire asked some tough questions—called 'voir dire'—to ensure you will objectively and fairly determine the defendant's guilt under the law, in accordance with the evidence, and that you will fairly choose between the only two penalties available under the law if you find the defendant guilty of murder by poisoning: life without the possibility of parole . . . or death."

The jurors, half male and half female, shifted nervously. Twelve regular jurors sat in the box, the six alternates in straight-backed wooden chairs in front of and below the jury box.

Judge Keefe made eye contact with each person.

"In your questionnaire you swore you hadn't formed an opinion about the death penalty that would impair your ability to be impartial. This applies equally to whether you might be personally predisposed to vote *for* or *against* the death penalty.

"I understand that since filling out your questionnaire and being selected to sit on the jury, two of you may have changed your minds. Would you please raise your hands."

An elderly man with white hair, wearing thick bifocals and a business suit, and a woman in her early twenties, wearing a long flowered dress and Birkenstocks, raised their hands.

"Juror Number Seven, what is your name?"

"Harold Macdonald."

"After *swearing* to be fair and impartial, why do you now believe you cannot be, Mr. Macdonald?"

He cleared his throat. "Last night I was thinking about my brother, who was murdered about thirty years ago. The man who killed him was convicted and sentenced to life in prison, but got out after only twenty years."

"How does that mean you can't be fair in this case?"

"Life without the possibility of parole doesn't mean what it says. Besides, the Bible says, 'an eye for an eye'—in my opinion, that's what convicted murderers deserve."

Keefe pursed his lips and contemplated. "Are you saying it would be impossible—not just difficult, but *impossible*—for you to judge this case impartially, based on the evidence and the law?"

"Well . . ."

"That if I instructed you on the law, you would *defy* my instructions?"

"Well . . ."

"You would *intentionally* dishonor your solemn oath?"

"I could probably be fair."

"Thank you, Mr. Macdonald, I knew you could."

Griffith stood. "I move to dismiss Juror Seven for cause."

"I'm satisfied Mr. Macdonald can be fair. There's no cause for dismissal."

Griffith objected. "A juror whose views would prevent or substantially impair the performance of his duties . . ."

Keefe flipped his hand. "I know the law."

"Judge . . ."

"I've made my ruling. I'm not going to let you stack the deck by excluding honest and impartial jurors, Mr. Griffith. Now sit down."

When Griffith sat, Kathryn whispered, "I thought we neutralized Keefe with your threat to call Fields."

"I thought so, too. He's more biased against you now than before I brought the motion."

"This isn't good. Macdonald sounds like he wants to be the one who sticks the needle in my arm. Use a peremptory challenge."

Griffith shook his head. "Can't, we're all out of peremptories."

Keefe turned to the jury box. "Juror Number Three, what is your name?"

"Bobbie Alderson."

"What's your problem?"

"I thought about it again last night. I guess I really don't believe in the death penalty."

"What does *that* mean?"

Alderson locked eyes with Keefe. "It means that since filling out my questionnaire, and looking at the defendant sitting there, there's no way I could vote for death."

"It would be impossible for you to judge this case impartially, based on the evidence?"

"That's not what I'm saying."

"If I instructed you about the law, you would *refuse* to obey me?"

"I might, with the death penalty at stake."

"The Court dismisses Juror Three for cause. Bailiff, seat an alternate in Ms. Alderson's place."

Once the alternate assumed the seat in the jury box, Keefe leaned forward, interlaced his fingers, and sat silently until every juror's eyes were on him.

"Ladies and gentlemen, you just witnessed the worst kind of dishonesty imaginable—a juror who solemnly swore to be fair, then, when faced with reality, reneged."

Keefe scowled. "If it were up to me, lying on a juror questionnaire would be punishable by jail. If there are other liars among you who swore on your questionnaires to be fair and impartial, but now intend to break that vow, speak up."

No one moved.

"Very well, then."

Keefe leaned back in his chair and smiled toward the jury box. "None of you is so predisposed for or against the death penalty to be precluded from weighing the possibility of that punishment. If that's right, raise your hands."

Every juror's hand went up.

Kathryn leaned close to Griffith. "Sounds like they're voting about where to go for pizza. We should've taken him on when he decided to voir dire the jury himself."

"A writ to the appellate court's a waste of time. It's his prerogative under the law."

"He should have voir dired each juror individually."

"Even if he did, and some gave equivocal answers to death-penalty questions, his determination about their state of mind is binding. By now they're too intimidated to give any answer except what he wants, anyway."

Keefe looked at the defense table. "The Court is satisfied with this jury. Court is adjourned until one-thirty this afternoon, when we will hear opening statements."

Kathryn looked at her lawyer. "The bastard empaneled a hanging jury."

CHAPTER
41

KEEFE WAITED until Kathryn and Griffith were seated at the defense table, then admitted the spectators and seated the jury.

He turned to the prosecution table. "Proceed with your opening statement."

"The prosecution waives opening statement."

"That's highly unusual, Mr. McCaskill."

"The evidence will speak for itself, Your Honor."

"Very well." Keefe turned to the defense table. "Mr. Griffith?"

Caught off guard, Roger Griffith walked slowly to the podium.

"Kathryn Mackay did not murder Robert Simmons," he whispered so softly that the jurors strained to hear.

He paused. "So, you're asking yourselves, 'If she didn't kill him, why is she on trial?' "

In a loud, confident voice, he answered himself: "Kathryn Mackay is on trial because this man"—he turned and pointed at McCaskill—"wants her job very badly, and to make sure he gets it for keeps, he's willing to kill her for it—and he wants you to do his dirty work for him by sentencing her to death.

"Don't let him get away with it.

"In eleven states," Griffith continued, "they considered it humane to electrocute people, until people learned that prison guards stood by with fire extinguishers in case the condemned person's burning flesh set the room ablaze.

"These days, we're led to believe it's humane to kill people by lethal injection. Don't believe it. All executions are gruesome.

"If Kathryn is convicted, Judge Keefe will set her execution date, and she'll be driven to San Quentin, where she'll be isolated from all human beings except the guards who will bring her food three times a day.

"Twenty-four hours before Kathryn's execution, guards will strip-search her, probe her body cavities, scan her with a metal detector, and give her clean clothes, move her to a death-watch cell a few feet down the hall, and the warden will ask what she wants to eat for her last meal."

The courtroom was silent except for an occasional cough, shuffling feet, and the whir of camera motors.

"Five minutes before Kathryn is executed, guards without name tags, and wearing face masks so no one knows who they are, will escort her to a preparation room beside the death chamber, where they will start two intravenous sterile saline IVs. As soon as the saline's flowing, they'll cover Kathryn with a sheet and roll her into the death chamber.

"Kathryn will be fully conscious. The warden will ask Kathryn if she has any last words.

"The saline lines will be shut off and sodium thiopental injected into Kathryn's veins, rendering her unconscious. Next, pancuronium bromide will be shot into Kathryn's arms to disable the nerves that control her body's voluntary muscles—her face, hands, legs, and lungs, causing her to stop breathing, but she won't be dead because her heart is an *involuntary* muscle that isn't affected by pancuronium bromide.

"Let's hope they're right about the sodium thiopental rendering her unconscious because if they're wrong—and medical evidence suggests they *are*—she'll know her lungs have stopped working and there's nothing she can do about it.

"Finally, potassium chloride will be injected into Kathryn's veins to interrupt electrical impulses from the brain to the heart. She'll suffer fatal cardiac arrest.

"When it's all over, society will be safe—protected from Kathryn Mackay—all five feet two, one hundred ten pounds of her, because she'll be gone."

He paused for several seconds. "Forever.

"After the prison doctor declares Kathryn dead, they'll wheel her body into a holding room, where her twelve-year-old daughter, Emma, can claim it.

"That's a hell of a harsh punishment for an innocent woman. And mark my words, by the end of this trial you will know in your hearts, and you will know in your minds, and you will know in your conscience that Kathryn Mackay is innocent."

CHAPTER

42

"PLEASE STATE YOUR NAME, and spell your last name for the court reporter."

"Mary Elizabeth Skinner, S-K-I-N-N-E-R." The first prosecution witness against Kathryn Mackay was in her midforties, tall and thin, pretty, with long glossy black hair tucked into a tight bun, bright blue eyes, and wore the sedate blue business suit that, for her, was almost a uniform. As usual, she wore very little makeup. Accustomed to asking rather than answering questions in Superior Court, she was visibly nervous.

"What is your occupation?" McCaskill asked.

"I'm Santa Rita County Chief Deputy District Attorney for Operations."

"How long have you been so employed?"

"About two and a half years. I was a staff attorney for twelve years before that."

"Then, you knew Kathryn Mackay before she became District Attorney?"

"Yes, she and I started in the DA's office at about the same time."

"How would you characterize your relationship with the defendant?"

"We were friends."

"Close friends?"

"As close as either of us had."

"Did the defendant aspire to be more than just an assistant DA for the rest of her career?"

"Objection." Griffith stood and leaned on the table with his palms. "The witness can't testify as to my client's thoughts."

"Sustained. Rephrase your question, Mr. McCaskill," Keefe directed.

"You and the defendant confided in each other?"

"Yes."

"Did she tell you she wanted to be *the* District Attorney someday?"

"Oh, yes."

"Did she say she was afraid she might never be DA because her boss, District Attorney Harold Benton, was so young?"

Skinner looked at the wall above the jurors' heads. "Yes."

"What about after the defendant became DA and made you her Chief Deputy?"

"We remained close friends, but worked more closely together than before, of course."

"So, you and the defendant still discussed personal matters, and she also consulted with you professionally?"

"Yes."

McCaskill stroked his chin, pretending to contemplate his next question. "Would it be fair to say that you knew the defendant better than anyone in the DA's office?"

"Objection," Griffith said. "The witness can't testify about how well someone else knew my client."

"I withdraw the question." McCaskill smiled at the jury, certain he had established exactly what Griffith said he shouldn't.

Then he changed directions. "Please tell the jury what happened two years ago on September first."

Skinner swallowed. "That was the Monday morning District Attorney Benton died of an apparent heart attack while he was having coffee with Doctor Robert Simmons."

"It was District Attorney Benton's sudden death that resulted in the defendant's appointment to District Attorney?"

"Yes."

"What was District Attorney Benton's relationship with Doctor Simmons?"

"They were friends. I saw them together frequently in the DA's office. They went to lunch together regularly, too."

"What did you mean a moment ago when you said District Attorney Benton died of an 'apparent' heart attack?"

"It appeared to be a heart attack at first, but blood

toxicology tests later determined that he died from a massive digitalis overdose."

"Really! Did he accidentally overdose himself, or deliberately commit suicide?"

"There was no evidence of either."

"No, of course not. Was anyone ever charged with his murder?"

"Yes. Kathryn eventually concluded that Doctor Simmons intentionally administered a fatal overdose of digitalis to District Attorney Benton."

"You mean the defendant, in her official capacity as District Attorney, concluded that Doctor Simmons murdered District Attorney Benton?"

"Yes."

"Did anyone see Doctor Simmons murder District Attorney Benton?"

"There were no eyewitnesses, if that's what you mean."

"That's what I meant. Did Doctor Simmons confess to murdering District Attorney Benton?"

"No."

"Then we don't know for sure who murdered District Attorney Benton by administering a massive digitalis overdose, do we?"

Griffith objected. "Calls for speculation by the witness."

"Overruled," Keefe shot back. "You may answer, Ms. Skinner."

"No, we don't know for sure who murdered him."

"It's possible, is it not, that anyone with access to the DA's inner offices, with whom District Attorney Benton knew well enough to share early-morning coffee, such as a high-level trusted assistant DA, could have administered a massive digitalis overdose?"

Griffith rose. "Your Honor, I object! The question calls for the witness to speculate on a matter about which she has no knowledge."

"Overruled, Mr. Griffith. I'm going to allow the prosecution to pursue this line of questioning."

He turned to the witness stand. "You may answer the question, Ms. Skinner."

"Yes, that's possible."

"Like the defendant, for example."

Skinner closed her eyes. "I suppose."

"And we'll never know if Doctor Simmons murdered his friend Hal Benton by slipping him a fatal overdose of digitalis, because Doctor Simmons has also been murdered by someone who slipped *him* a massive digitalis overdose, right?"

"Objection."

"Overruled. Answer the question, Ms. Skinner."

"That's right," Skinner responded.

"Okay. A few questions back, you said the defendant 'eventually' charged Doctor Simmons with the murder. How long after the murder of District Attorney Benton were charges filed?"

"About a month."

"That long!"

Kathryn leaned toward Griffith and placed her lips close to his ear so no one would overhear. "McCaskill hasn't charged a murder in less than six months in his whole career."

Griffith patted her hand, but didn't reply.

"Between the time District Attorney Benton was

murdered and when the defendant filed charges against Doctor Simmons, do you have personal knowledge of whether or not the defendant became involved in a romantic relationship with Doctor Simmons?"

Skinner drew in a deep breath and shifted in the chair. "Yes, they were having an affair. Kathryn told me she was seeing him, and that they went to Victoria, British Columbia, together for a weekend."

"Do you know how long after District Attorney Benton was murdered that the defendant went away with Doctor Simmons?"

"It was the next weekend."

"Four days after her boss was murdered!"

"Yes."

"How can you be so sure today it was that soon?"

"I remember thinking that it was unusual for Kathryn to be so—spontaneous."

"Did you ever ask the defendant about her strange behavior?"

"No, I figured if she wanted to talk to me about it, she would."

"And, did she?"

"No."

"All right. Now, Ms. Skinner, let's fast-forward from the day District Attorney Benton was murdered to just before charges were filed against Doctor Simmons by the defendant. To your knowledge, were she and Doctor Simmons still—let me put this as delicately as possible—romantically involved at that time?"

"No, she told me she had stopped seeing him a

couple of weeks after their trip to Victoria because she was conducting a criminal investigation of one of his clinics."

"I see. She didn't tell you that Doctor Simmons had broken off the relationship?"

"No, she said she had broken it off because she didn't want it to appear there was a conflict of interest while the investigation was under way."

"But she didn't think it looked funny that she had become sexually involved with the man whom only two weeks later she accused of killing her boss?"

"Your Honor, I object, argumentative!" Griffith shouted.

"Sustained." Keefe checked the clock. "It's almost time for the lunch break. I assume you have more questions for this witness, Mr. McCaskill?"

"Oh, indeed I do, Your Honor."

"Then we'll recess and reconvene at one-thirty this afternoon."

Griffith turned to his client. "Should I order sandwiches?"

"I'm not hungry."

"You need to eat."

"McCaskill just accused me of killing Benton *and* Simmons. And my own Chief Deputy, not to mention my so-called friend, helped him do it."

"You expected kindergarten kickball rules? How many times have you or one of your prosecutors done the same thing to one of my clients?"

"Whose side are you on?"

"Yours. This is just round one. We get our chance in round two."

CHAPTER

43

"Ms. SKINNER," McCaskill said, "before we broke for lunch you testified that the defendant told you she stopped seeing Doctor Simmons because she was conducting a criminal investigation of one of his clinics, is that right?"

"Yes."

"Please describe the nature of that investigation."

"One of the clinic doctors raped several of his teenage female patients, and then, when he learned one of them was pregnant with his child, he aborted the fetus, but she died."

"You said 'patients.' How many teenage girls did this doctor rape?"

"Five or six. I don't recall the exact number today."

"Doctor Robert Simmons committed these rapes and killed that girl?"

"No, it was one of his staff physicians, Doctor Eduardo Berroa."

"Was Doctor Simmons implicated in the crimes?"

"That was never determined for certain, to my knowledge. District Attorney Benton's confidential investigation file—he called them 'R-files'—indicated that Doctor Simmons offered to assist in the investigation."

"Did he?"

"District Attorney Benton was murdered before he could."

"According to the defendant, by Doctor Simmons, right?"

"Yes."

"Did the defendant allege that Doctor Simmons committed any other crimes?"

"She accused him of intentionally overdosing her on digitalis, as well."

McCaskill looked around the courtroom and scratched his head. "I see the defendant sitting there, and she doesn't look dead to me. Can you explain that?"

"She was hospitalized and treated."

"So, the dosage of digitalis Doctor Simmons allegedly administered to District Attorney Benton was fatal, but the dosage the defendant contends he administered to her wasn't, is that correct?"

"Yes."

"Did the treating physician at the hospital determine, to your knowledge, that Doctor Simmons administered digitalis to the defendant?"

"No, she was treated by her friend, Doctor Nelson."

"I see. Given your knowledge of the defendant, would you agree with me that she might have overdosed herself, to make it look like Doctor Simmons tried to murder her?"

Griffith rose. "I object again to this line of questioning, which calls for the witness to speculate on matters about which she has no personal knowledge."

"Overruled, Mr. Griffith. I'm going to allow it." Keefe turned to the witness stand. "Answer the question, Ms. Skinner."

"I suppose it's possible, yes."

"All right, let's go back. How did the defendant discover the crimes Doctor Berroa committed?"

"She found the R-file."

"Ah yes, the R-file. Was Doctor Berroa sentenced to prison for the murder and rapes?"

Skinner shook her head. "He was charged and convicted of involuntary manslaughter."

McCaskill cupped his hand over his ear. "Excuse me, I thought you said that after Doctor Berroa raped half a dozen teenage girls, even killed one of them, he got off with a slap on the wrist—involuntary manslaughter. Did I hear you right?"

"Yes."

"How could something like that happen?"

"The defendant made a deal with Doctor Berroa. He would testify that Doctor Simmons admitted to him that he murdered District Attorney Benton. In exchange, Kathryn didn't charge him with the rapes."

McCaskill turned toward the jury. "But, surely the

defendant charged Doctor Berroa for the murder of the young woman who died from the botched abortion!"

"The defendant charged him with involuntary manslaughter."

"You were Chief Deputy DA when the defendant charged Doctor Berroa?"

"I was."

"Did you express concern to the defendant about the deal she cut and the charges she filed?"

"I discussed with her the fact that involuntary manslaughter carries only a two- to four-year sentence."

"What did she say?"

"She said, 'It's not a perfect world.' "

McCaskill stared at Skinner and shook his head slowly, turned and stared at Kathryn, then finally stared at the jury and shook his head again. Then he walked back to the prosecution table, thumbed through a stack of papers, and returned to the podium.

"Well, at least Doctor Berroa's testimony led to the arrest of Doctor Simmons for murdering District Attorney Benton, right?"

"It led to a Grand Jury indictment, but Doctor Simmons had fled the country before the deal was cut," Skinner said.

"Did the defendant know to where Doctor Simmons had fled?"

"No."

"Doctor Berroa is in prison for involuntary manslaughter, though, is that correct?"

"No, Doctor Berroa escaped from Soledad State Prison about three months ago."

"Has he been captured?"

"No."

"So the defendant cut a deal with a killer and rapist of teenage girls, sent him to prison for a couple of years, he escaped and is now prowling our streets. All so she could indict a man she *alleged* but couldn't prove murdered District Attorney Benton, and *alleged* but couldn't prove, tried unsuccessfully to kill her, even though she had no idea where that man was, or whether he would ever be captured, is that correct?"

Skinner shifted in her chair, crossed her left leg over her right, then uncrossed them and leaned forward. "I suppose you could put it that way."

McCaskill glared at her. "Would you prefer to put it some other way, Ms. Skinner?"

She looked at her lap. "No."

"I didn't think so. I only have a few more questions, so let's move on. Was Doctor Simmons' whereabouts ever determined before he was arrested in Spain?"

"Yes. About a year and a half ago, Kathryn received information that he was in Costa Rica. She flew there and had him arrested."

"She flew there personally, rather than requesting that Costa Rican police take him into custody, or sending one of her inspectors. As Chief Deputy, did you consider that a wise decision at the time?"

"No. We were investigating a series of infant kidnappings at the time, and it wasn't her job."

"Did you advise her of that?"

"Of what?"

"That you thought her decision unwise, Ms. Skinner!"

"No."

"Why not?"

Skinner pleaded with McCaskill with her eyes and didn't answer, but he continued to stare at her.

"Ms. Skinner, tell the jury why you did not advise the defendant that it was unwise to trot off to Costa Rica."

"I didn't think she would listen."

"Why not?"

"I . . ."

"Didn't you tell me it was because you thought the defendant had become so obsessed with Doctor Simmons that her judgment was seriously impaired?"

"Yes," Skinner whispered.

"Speak up so the jury and court reporter can hear your answer."

Skinner looked at McCaskill. Her eyes had begun to fill with tears. "Yes."

"All right. If the defendant arrested Doctor Simmons in Costa Rica a year and a half or so ago, why did she go to Spain and arrest him again?"

"He escaped."

"From whose custody?"

"Costa Rican prison authorities."

"Did the defendant tell you how he escaped?"

"In her extradition request, Kathryn wouldn't waive the death penalty, and Costa Rica is a non-capital-punishment country. She said Costa Rican politicians arranged his escape in order to prevent a diplomatic incident."

"She must have wanted him dead pretty bad, wouldn't you say?"

"Your Honor!"

"Sit down, Mr. Griffith, your objection is sustained."

"Withdrawn," McCaskill conceded. "Ms. Skinner, Spain is also a non-capital-punishment country, isn't it?"

"Yes."

"Why do you suppose Doctor Simmons didn't 'escape' from Spain's custody as well?"

Griffith stood. "Objection!"

"I'll allow it," Keefe ruled. "You may answer the question, Ms. Skinner."

"Kathryn waived the death penalty before Doctor Simmons was extradited from Spain."

"She did? That means when she left Spain with Doctor Simmons in her custody, she knew he would never die by lethal injection for allegedly murdering District Attorney Benton, right?"

"Yes."

"And that if he was *ever* to die, she would have to take matters into her own hands, execute him herself, before that airplane landed in San Francisco?"

Griffith jumped up.

Before he could voice his objection, McCaskill said, "Withdrawn. No further questions."

Keefe checked the clock, then looked at the defense table. "Mr. Griffith, it's approaching time to adjourn for the day. I assume you'd prefer to start your cross-examination tomorrow morning?"

"Yes, Your Honor."

After the jury was escorted from the room, and Keefe left the bench, Griffith asked the bailiff to allow him a few minutes with his client.

"We need to talk, Kathryn."

"What's there to talk about? Skinner buried me alive. With friends like her, I don't need any more enemies."

"It wasn't good," Griffith conceded. "We need Emma here tomorrow."

Kathryn shook her head. "I won't take her out of school, she needs normalcy in her life. And the last thing she needs to hear is McCaskill making me sound like Jack the Ripper."

"I understand, but if I don't create some sympathy on that jury, that's how *they'll* see you. I need Emma sitting behind you while I cross-examine Skinner."

"No."

"Saying 'no' might be a fatal mistake." Griffith grabbed his papers, stuffed them into his briefcase, slammed it shut, and motioned for the bailiff. "I'll come by the jail after dinner."

"Not tonight. Dave arranged for Emma to visit me in his lieutenant's office in the jail."

Griffith set his briefcase on the table. "Kathryn, if the guilt phase of this trial ended today, I couldn't save you from a death sentence."

"I have to see Emma." Kathryn stood and extended her wrists to the bailiff, who handcuffed her, then grasped her elbow.

She turned back to her lawyer. "Roger, do you do adoptions?"

He shook his head. "It's highly specialized."

"Do you know an attorney who does?"

"Yes, why?"

"Just wondering."

CHAPTER

44

"PUT THESE ON." Dave Granz pulled the door closed and handed Kathryn a Safeway bag.

She glanced inside. "Street clothes. Thanks."

"Figured some normal time might be good for you and Emma."

"As normal as possible, anyway." She glanced around his lieutenant's office, whose windows were crisscrossed by metal bars. "Where is she?"

"Talking to Deputy Martinez at the booking desk. Her homework assignment is to interview someone in Spanish. She's asking Martinez about her hobby."

"Which is?"

"Hang gliding. Believe me, when Martinez starts on that subject, she'll talk your ear off. I told her I'd come get Emma when we're ready."

Kathryn pulled a pair of J.Crew jeans and a dark blue T-shirt from the bag, spread the shirt on the desk, and started smoothing the wrinkles with her hand.

"What's new on the Tucker murder investigation?" she asked.

"Nada. I'm at a dead end now that Keefe and Sanchez have been cleared."

"Has CSI determined how the killer got into the building?"

"No, it's like he materialized out of thin air, murdered her, then vaporized without a trace. I'm gonna have to put it on the back burner unless something turns up soon."

He pointed at the bag. "There's more in there."

She pulled out a red bra and bikini panties.

"Better change," he told her. "I'll close my eyes."

"Keep them open. You haven't looked at me in a long time." She unzipped the jumpsuit and slid it off, then unfastened her bra, dropped it to the floor, and stepped out of her panties.

"Don't tease," he told her.

"I'm not teasing."

"We don't have much time."

"We don't need much time."

She unzipped his Levi's and pulled them down, pushed him into the chair, and slid her mouth over him. After a moment, she straddled him and slowly lowered herself until she consumed him.

Dave kissed each breast. "I was hungry for you."

"I was *starving*." She raised and lowered her body slowly, and he arched his back to meet her.

When they were finished, Kathryn whispered, "I wish we could stay like this forever, but . . ." She freed herself from his arms, slipped on the red underwear, then her jeans and T-shirt, while he watched.

Dave stood up and dressed. "I'll get Emma."

CHAPTER

45

"Hi, Mom."

Kathryn hugged her daughter. "I'm so glad to see you."

"Lupe said she'd take me hang gliding someday."

"Lupe?"

"Deputy Martinez. Her name's Lupe."

Kathryn shook her head. "That sounds pretty dangerous, sweetie."

"Oh, Mom, you're such a sissy! We women can do dangerous things nowadays."

"Let's talk about it later. How's school going?"

"Fine, 'cept in math we're doing polynomial equations. They're hard, and we have a test tomorrow. Dave's gonna help me when we get home."

"Glad to hear it, I'm not very good at math."

"I need help with English, too, Mom. I brought my book. Will you?"

Kathryn faked a sneeze so she could turn her head and wipe the tears from her eyes. "Of course, honey. Let's spread your homework out on Lieutenant Aldridge's desk." She glanced at Dave for approval.

He nodded and winked. "I don't know an adjective from an elbow. You two work on it. I need to go to my office and make some phone calls."

He checked to be sure Emma wasn't watching, then pointed at his watch and silently mouthed, *One hour.*

Kathryn blew him a discreet kiss.

He mouthed, *I love you.*

CHAPTER

46

DAVE KNOCKED on Aldridge's door, waited a moment, then entered. Emma was just tucking her homework into her backpack.

"How'd the English go?" he asked.

Emma shrugged. "I think I can conjugate verbs pretty good now."

"Well," Dave corrected.

"Well what?" Emma asked.

Dave and Kathryn both laughed. "Forget it. By the way, Em, Lupe says there's something she forgot to mention. Asked that you stop by before we leave. Why don't you go see what's on her mind while I tell your mom good night. I'll be there in five minutes."

" 'Kay." Emma threw her arms around Kathryn's neck and clung. "Hurry and come home."

"I love you so much, honey." Kathryn didn't try to hide her anguish. "But remember, Dave loves you, too."

"And I love him, but I don't love anyone as much as you, Mom."

Dave placed his hand gently on Emma's shoulder. She gave Kathryn a last squeeze and stood up. "Bye, Mom."

CHAPTER

47

KATHRYN LEANED AGAINST DAVE until her sobs subsided. "If I lose control, I'll never get it back."

"Take your time, Babe."

"All the years I've been a prosecutor, I've been a staunch advocate of capital punishment. I didn't think it was possible to sentence an innocent person to death. I was wrong. They're going to execute me."

"Griffith hasn't put on your defense yet."

"What defense? Skinner stuck the needle in my arm. McCaskill just needs someone to push in the plunger on the syringe."

"Griffith'll blast holes in her testimony big enough to sail a battleship through. You're being pessimistic."

"I'm being realistic. I've got to face it, and—"

"Babe . . ."

"Let me finish. And so do you. I need to ask you something, but you must promise to not answer until you think it over."

"Kate . . ."

"Please."

"I promise."

"Emma loves you, Dave. You're the only family she knows. When I'm convicted, I want you to adopt her, if you're willing."

"Kate . . ."

"You promised you wouldn't say anything until you think it over."

"There's nothing to think over, you know I'm willing. But, you're not going to be convicted."

"Yes I am."

CHAPTER
48

"How would you define 'friend,' Ms. Skinner?"

Roger Griffith leaned casually against the podium, left hand in the pants pocket of his dark brown suit, right hand on a stack of dictionaries.

"Excuse me?"

"Tell the jury how you define the word 'friend.' "

She contemplated. "I'm not sure."

Griffith lifted his hands, palms up. "That's obvious from your testimony about my client."

"Objection!" McCaskill said. "Argumentative."

Keefe shot Griffith a dirty look. "Sustained."

"Let's see if I can help." Griffith flipped the *American Heritage Dictionary* open to a page marked with a yellow Post-it. " 'A person whom one knows, likes, and trusts.' Is that how you'd describe a friend?"

"I suppose."

He opened the *Cambridge International.* "If you're not sure, how about this one: 'Someone who is not an enemy, and whom you can trust'? Or *Merriam-Webster's* definition: 'One that is not hostile'?"

"Are you planning to make a point in the not-too-distant future, Mr. Griffith?" Keefe asked.

"If the Court will give me some latitude."

Keefe sighed. "Answer the question, Ms. Skinner."

Skinner had on a suit almost identical to the one she had worn the previous day. She shifted in her chair and absently tugged at her dark blue skirt as she considered her answer. "I suppose I agree with those definitions of 'friend.' "

"Please share with the jury the argument you had with Kathryn Mackay."

"What argument?"

"The argument that ended your friendship."

"We didn't have an argument."

"A serious difference of professional opinion?"

"We rarely disagreed on professional matters."

"Then you still consider Kathryn Mackay a friend?"

"Yes."

"Interesting. Then, you must agree with Oscar Wilde that 'A true friend stabs you in the front.' "

McCaskill jumped up. Before he could object, Griffith said, "Withdrawn."

"Ms. Skinner, you testified that my client once said she feared she'd never be District Attorney because her boss, Harold Benton, was so young."

"Yes."

"When did she say that?"

"I don't recall, exactly."

"Approximately's close enough."

"I don't recall."

"Where were you when she shared this intimate personal thought with you?"

"I don't recall."

"Uh-huh. You don't remember *when* she said it, or *where* she said it, you just remember she said it, right?"

"Yes."

Griffith pursed his lips and shook his head sadly, then looked at the jury.

"Mr. McCaskill did prepare you for yesterday and today's testimony, right?"

"Yes."

"More than once?"

"Yes."

"More than five times?"

"Your Honor!" McCaskill objected.

"The Court gets the point, Mr. Griffith. Move on."

"And it was Mr. McCaskill who suggested to you that Kathryn said she'd never be DA because of Harold Benton's age, right?"

"I don't remember."

"So it's possible my client *never* made that statement at all, but that Mr. McCaskill told you to say she did?"

"No, I'm sure she said it." Skinner's voice rose, as if asking a question rather than making a statement.

"Since, as you testified, you rarely disagreed with Kathryn on professional matters, it's accurate to say you agreed with her that DA Benton died of a digitalis overdose administered immediately before his apparent heart attack?"

"Doctor Nelson rendered that opinion, not Kathryn."

Griffith held up a piece of paper. "The same Doctor Nelson who appears on Mr. McCaskill's witness list as an expert on forensic pathology and toxicology?"

"Yes."

"Whose forensic opinion was that ex-DA Benton was administered enough digitalis to—" he picked up another document and read from it, 'stop his heart almost instantly.' "

"Yes."

"The Sheriff's investigation showed Doctor Simmons was with the District Attorney when he had the apparent heart attack and that, in fact, Kathryn was with Doctor Nelson at the morgue when it occurred, right?"

"Doctor Nelson's her best friend."

"Didn't you testify that you're her best friend?"

"I said I'm her *close* friend."

"As close as either of you had, right?" He paused. "Are you saying Mr. McCaskill's expert witness might lie?"

Skinner tugged absently at the hem of her skirt, then clasped her hands in her lap. "I didn't say that."

"Good. Did you tell Kathryn that in your professional opinion, Doctor Simmons didn't murder ex-DA Benton?"

"No."

"That you thought she should waive the death penalty against Robert Simmons?"

"No."

"That she shouldn't make a deal with Doctor Berroa, whose crimes were less serious, to allow Berroa to testify before the Grand Jury?"

"No."

Griffith continued. "You were Chief Deputy when Kathryn charged Doctor Berroa with involuntary manslaughter, and you and she discussed the fact that involuntary manslaughter carries only a two- to four-year sentence. Did you tell Kathryn you thought it was a bad idea?"

"No."

"As Chief Deputy District Attorney, is it your professional opinion today, that it was a bad idea?"

"I'm not sure."

"Did you tell Kathryn you didn't think she should personally extradite Robert Simmons from Costa Rica?"

"No, but as I testified, we were investigating a series of infant kidnappings at the time."

"In fact, that investigation hadn't been turned over by the Sheriff to the District Attorney's office at the time Kathryn traveled to Costa Rica, isn't that correct?"

"Yes, that's correct."

"Who was Chief Deputy before my client elevated you to that position?"

"Neal McCaskill."

Griffith pointed to the prosecution table. "*This* Neal McCaskill, who is now your boss?"

"Yes."

"What happened to McCaskill when you replaced him?"

"Kathryn assigned him to misdemeanors, and later fired him."

"For what?"

"Insubordination."

"That's all?"

Skinner implored McCaskill with her eyes, but he didn't look at her.

"Should I repeat the question?" Griffith insisted.

"Insubordination and violating office policy against politicking on county time. Did you agree with Kathryn's decision to fire McCaskill?"

"Yes," she said softly.

"Was McCaskill aware of that?"

"Yes."

Griffith puckered his lips and whistled softly. "That must've pissed—excuse me, that must've made him angry at both of you!"

Before McCaskill could react, he said, "Withdrawn. The Chief Deputy position you hold is at-will, that is, you don't enjoy civil service protection, is that right?"

"Yes."

"When Mr. McCaskill was appointed Interim DA pending Kathryn's exoneration, did you think he might retaliate against you?"

"I considered the possibility."

"But, you're still Chief Deputy, right?"

"That's right."

"Because McCaskill promised you'd remain his

Chief Deputy if you testified against my client, and if you didn't, you wouldn't, right?"

"I—"

McCaskill's face turned red and he leaped from his chair. "Sidebar, Your Honor!"

Keefe wiggled his fingers. "Counsel may approach."

"Judge," McCaskill protested, "the defense has no right to delve into irrelevant private conversations I had with one of my employees."

"There's no such thing as employer-employee privilege, and McCaskill wasn't her lawyer, so there's no attorney-client privilege," Griffith said. "If Skinner was coerced, it bears on her credibility as a witness, and I have a right to cross-examine her on it."

Keefe thought for a moment. "I'm afraid Mr. Griffith's right. I'm going to allow him to pursue this line of questioning. Now, step back."

After the court reporter read back the question, Skinner said, "He didn't say it in so many words, but he implied that I might be disciplined."

"Disciplined how?"

"Demoted or fired."

"So, to protect your job, you agreed to lie if necessary to convict Kathryn of murder?"

"I never promised to lie."

"To your knowledge, as Kathryn's close friend, did my client drink to excess?"

"Not to my knowledge."

"Use illegal drugs?"

"No."

"Abuse prescription drugs?"

"Not to my knowledge."

"Suffer from depression?"

McCaskill stood. "The witness isn't a doctor and can't opine on the defendant's emotional condition."

Griffith smiled. "I'll rephrase. Did my client ever tell you she was depressed?"

"No."

"That life wasn't worth living?"

"No."

"That she didn't care about watching her daughter, Emma, grow up?"

"No."

"That she might commit suicide?"

"No."

"So, to your knowledge, there's no rational basis for believing Kathryn intentionally overdosed herself on digitalis?"

Skinner looked at Kathryn for the first time. "Not unless she wanted to make it look like Doctor Simmons had tried to kill her."

Griffith stopped, started to speak, but didn't. Kathryn clenched her fists and squeezed her eyes shut.

"No further questions."

When Griffith sat down, Kathryn slid her chair close. "Jesus Christ, Roger!" Kathryn's voice rose. "McCaskill must've coached her to not appear reticent, to look like she's just doing her duty by answering questions and telling the truth. He anticipated that last question, wrote out the answer for her, and ordered her to practice until she recited it in her sleep."

"You're right, that's what I'd've done."

"And you walked into it like a goddamn brainless insect flies without looking into a Venus flytrap."

"I screwed up asking her that last question."

"You sure did, and you might as well have rolled my gurney into the death chamber."

CHAPTER

49

"EVERYTHING OKAY, EM? You haven't talked since we got here, or eaten a bite."

"We used to come here with Mom on Fridays."

Dave set the half-eaten burrito on his plate and glanced around Sophia's Taqueria, which was almost empty. "I know, it was—it's our favorite place."

"I miss her."

"Me, too. Is that why you're so quiet?"

"I s'pose."

"Did something happen at school today?"

Emma dipped a chip in the fiery hot red salsa, nibbled it, and sipped her Coke. "Yeah."

"Wanna talk about it?"

Emma pulled the crumpled front page of that morning's newspaper headline from her backpack and handed it to him.

EX-DA GOES ON TRIAL
Friday March 15

This morning, District Attorney Neal McCaskill will call his first witness against ex-DA Kathryn Mackay, who is accused of murdering ex-lover and County Health Officer Robert Simmons. Sources close to the DA say the first prosecution witness will be Mackay's close friend, Chief Deputy DA Mary Skinner.

McCaskill says he is confident that the evidence against Mackay will lead to a conviction for murder with special circumstances and execution in San Quentin's death chamber. . . .

"Where'd you get this?" Dave asked.

Tears welled in her brown eyes, ran down her freckled cheeks, and dripped onto her cheese quesadilla. "Someone taped it to my locker during lunch. I hate them!"

"Hate who?"

"All the kids at my school."

"It was only one kid, Em, you can't be angry at everyone. Besides, your mom needs our help to get through this, and you can't help her if you're angry. Can you put your anger behind you for her sake?"

"I'll try."

"I know you will." Dave walked around the table, pulled her close, and stroked her hair. "Did you tell the principal about it?"

"No."

"How come?"

" 'Cause she prob'ly thinks Mom killed Doctor Simmons, too. 'Convicted' means 'guilty,' huh?"

"Yeah."

She freed herself and sat up straight. "If she's convicted, will they . . ."

She pointed to the words *execution in San Quentin's death chamber*, which someone had underlined in red.

Dave ripped the paper into tiny pieces and wadded them up. "I don't know."

"Let's ask Mr. Griffith."

"He won't know, either, Em. If she's convicted, it'll be up to the jury."

"Mom wouldn't kill anyone. You have to prove she didn't do it." Tears welled in her eyes again and she grabbed his hand.

He started to shake his head.

"Mom said you're the best detective she ever knew."

"I'm not sure . . ."

"You can do it. Please! Me and you're all Mom's got!"

"Emma—all right."

"Can we visit her tomorrow?"

"Sure."

"Sunday, too?"

"Absolutely, Sunday too."

CHAPTER
50

AFTER THEY LEFT Sophia's, Dave drove to Baskin-Robbins, then to Ashley's to bring her home for a sleepover.

Dave had moved Emma's furniture into his spare bedroom, painted it powder blue, and installed a separate telephone line, trying to make her feel at home, but he wasn't sure he'd succeeded. He had no such doubts about her yellow Lab. Sam had trotted from room to room, sniffing every inch of the house, then plopped down in Emma's room, staking it out as his territory.

They were eating ice-cream and watching television when the phone rang. Sam followed Dave into the kitchen, hoping for a taste of the French vanilla.

"Granz."

"Roger Griffith. You heard about Skinner's testimony today?"

"Yeah, Kate said it didn't go too well."

"Gross understatement. And I've got more bad news."

"Why doesn't that surprise me?"

"I lost my motion to keep you off the witness stand."

"Shit!" Granz slammed his fist on the countertop.

Sam cringed, so he set his ice-cream bowl on the floor.

"What the hell happened to the privilege to not testify against my wife?"

"Keefe ruled McCaskill could call you as a witness under an exception to the privilege."

"What exception?"

"McCaskill claims Kathryn planned in advance to murder Simmons, and married you so you couldn't testify against her if it came to trial. Keefe says it fits under Evidence Code section 972-F."

"That's bullshit. I've got a privilege to refuse to disclose communications made in confidence between Kate and me while we were husband and wife."

"There's no privilege if the communication was intended to enable someone to commit a crime."

"More legal bullshit. I didn't aid or abet any fucking murder."

"The exception's broader than that."

"Appeal Keefe's ruling."

"Wouldn't do any good. You're gonna have to testify, just don't help the son of a bitch."

"Count on it."

"I need you to do something for us."

"Name it."

"The attendant on that flight from London no longer works for British Air, and my investigator ran into a dead end. Find her."

"What for? She's not on McCaskill's witness list."

"That's what bothers me."

"What'd she tell his inspectors?"

"Nobody cut a report on an interview with her. Or if they did, they're keeping it from me."

"Maybe they couldn't find her, either."

"McCaskill wouldn't let that slide. He talked to her, all right."

"Mac's not stupid enough to break the discovery laws."

"Stupid no, but he hates Kathryn enough to do just about anything. If he talked to that stew, I want to know what she told him."

Granz thought. "Your investigator didn't find out where she went from British Air?"

"They won't give us that information without a court order, and I can't get one over the weekend."

"I'll bet she's still flying—how about the other carriers?"

"They won't tell him anything, either, but they'll cooperate with you, you're law enforcement. If you don't locate her, nobody can."

"I'll try."

"Trying's not good enough. My gut instinct tells me Kathryn's case depends on what that stew has to say."

"I'll find her."

"You'd better, because Kathryn's case is headed down the toilet, and right now I can't save her."

CHAPTER

51

GRANZ WAITED until the jurors had filed in and were settling into their chairs before he rushed into the courtroom, leaned over the railing between the spectators and the defense table, and kissed Kathryn.

"You look pretty."

Kathryn was wearing a new light gray Gianni pants suit with a black silk blouse that Dave and Emma had bought for her at Macy's, and shown her for approval Saturday at the jail. Her hair was brushed straight back, and her makeup was flawless.

"Thanks." She held his hand. "I felt so awful after Mary Elizabeth's testimony last Friday, but seeing you and Em over the weekend helped a lot."

He patted her shoulder and slipped a paper to Roger Griffith.

Griffith read it quickly. "You located the flight attendant?"

"Yeah, she's flying for Air Canada out of Vancouver, B.C. I'll track her down once I'm through testifying."

CHAPTER

52

"PLEASE STATE YOUR FULL NAME, and spell your last name for the court reporter," McCaskill said.

"David Granz, G-R-A-N-Z."

"What is your occupation?"

"Santa Rita County Sheriff-Coroner."

"When were you elected to that position?"

"November of last year."

"How long have you been a peace officer?"

"More than twenty years."

"Has all your law enforcement experience been in Santa Rita County?"

"Yes."

"Describe that experience for the jury, please."

"I was Sheriff's Chief of Detectives before I ran for office, and a DA Investigator before that. Previously, I was a street cop—a Sheriff's patrol deputy."

"During your more than twenty years as a peace officer, has the prosecution ever called you to testify in court?"

"Many times."

"On those occasions, did you meet with the prosecutors to discuss your testimony before testifying in court?"

"Yes."

"Did you receive requests to meet and discuss today's testimony with me before appearing?"

"Yes."

"What was your response to those requests?"

"I refused to meet with you."

"That's right, you did, so let's get right to the reason for those refusals. You're acquainted with the defendant, correct?"

"Yes."

"Describe your relationship to the defendant."

Granz looked at Kathryn before answering. "She's my wife."

"When were you married?"

"The morning of January twelfth."

"The day Doctor Robert Simmons was murdered?"

"The day he died."

"Right. With whom does the defendant's twelve-year-old daughter live while her mother is in custody on murder charges?"

"Me."

"How did that come about?"

"It's what Emma, Kathryn, and I felt was best, and what the juvenile court ordered, as you know."

McCaskill turned to the bench. "In view of the witness's bias resulting from his relationship with the defendant, permission to examine Sheriff Granz as a hostile witness."

Keefe nodded. "Granted."

"You're aware that the defendant once had a romantic and sexual affair with Doctor Robert Simmons, are you not?"

"Yes."

"You're also aware that just days after Judge Jemima Tucker was murdered, the defendant claims she received an anonymous tip about Doctor Simmons' whereabouts?"

"Yes."

"You and she flew to Spain together to apprehend him, despite the urgency of the Tucker murder investigation?"

"If we hadn't, my detective and her investigator would have been pulled off the Tucker investigation."

"Because of Judge Tucker's prominent position, didn't you consider her murder a high-priority investigation?"

Granz leaned forward in the witness chair. "They're all high-priority investigations, no matter who the victim is."

McCaskill turned to Keefe. "Judge, please instruct the witness to answer the question rather than make a speech."

"The witness is so admonished. Continue."

"When you and the defendant arrived in Torremolinos, Doctor Simmons was in Spanish police custody, right?"

"Yes."

"You interviewed Doctor Simmons?"

"Yes."

"You consulted with the defendant before and during that interview?"

"Yes."

McCaskill flipped through a yellow legal pad. "Your report says Doctor Simmons agreed to be extradited if the defendant agreed not to seek the death penalty, is that right?"

"That's right."

"You recommended she make that agreement?"

"Yes."

"In fact, you talked her into it, didn't you?"

Dave hesitated. "We discussed it."

"All right. Would you say that at first, she was reluctant to accept his offer?"

"I'd say so."

"And after you discussed it with her, she finally agreed?"

"That's right."

"Was she reluctant because she wanted very badly for Doctor Simmons to die?"

"You'd have to ask her."

"Uh-huh. You had a conversation with Chief Deputy Skinner, in her office, the day after you and the defendant returned from Spain?"

Granz shifted in the chair and glanced at Skinner, who sat at the prosecution table beside McCaskill.

"Yes."

"During that conversation, did Ms. Skinner express surprise, and ask how you convinced her boss to waive the death penalty against Doctor Simmons?"

"She asked if I knew why."

"Did you tell her that during your interview of Doctor Robert Simmons in the jail at Torremolinos, you talked the defendant into waiving the death penalty?"

"I didn't talk her into it."

"That wasn't the question—I asked whether or not you *told* Chief Deputy Skinner you talked her into it."

"I might have."

"And that before you discussed it with her, the defendant was very reluctant to waive the death penalty, agreeing only after she talked with you at considerable length?"

"It's possible I told her that."

Griffith shook his head. "Didn't you also tell Ms. Skinner that you became exasperated with the defendant and told her she couldn't be Doctor Simmons' judge, jury, and executioner?"

Granz turned his eyes to the defense table, hoping an objection would prevent him from walking into McCaskill's trap, but he knew no help would come.

"Yes."

"What did you tell Chief Deputy Skinner the defendant said in response to your admonition?"

Dave looked at Kathryn, closed his eyes, and reopened them slowly. "That she said, '*Yes I can.*' "

"Just two more questions, Sheriff. You and the defendant were married the morning following the conversation that you related to Chief Deputy Skinner, is that right?"

"Yes."

"And Doctor Robert Simmons was murdered later that same day?"

"He died later that same day."

McCaskill stared at the jury for several seconds, then turned to the bench. "No more questions at this time."

"May this witness be excused?" Keefe asked.

"No, Your Honor, I plan to recall this witness."

CHAPTER

53

"Jesus, Dave, why did you tell Skinner about our conversation at Torremolinos?"

Kathryn, wearing her maroon jumpsuit, leaned forward on the jail watch commander's desk, one hand under her chin, the other holding the phone.

"I forgot about that conversation until McCaskill brought it up. She was surprised you agreed to waive the death penalty and asked how I talked you into it. I had no idea at the time that she'd roll over on you."

"I should hope not! How'd McCaskill find out?"

Granz shifted the phone to his left hand, lay back on the bed, and propped his head up on the pillows.

"Probably gave it up to McCaskill when the evidence against you mounted."

"Where are you?"

"Vancouver, B.C."

"Have you talked to the flight attendant yet?"

He shook his head, then realized she couldn't see him. "No, by the time I cleared Customs, it was too late. I checked into the Wedgewood Hotel downtown. First thing tomorrow, I'll try to hook up with her, see what she has to say."

"Let's hope it's something good."

"It'll never repair the damage I did today. I'm sorry."

"You couldn't have known McCaskill would get his hands on your notes." She changed subjects. "Emma's at Ruth's?"

"Yeah."

Kathryn was silent for several seconds. "Hurry home. I'm lonely knowing you're away."

"I love you, Kate."

"I know. Dave, I'm scared."

"I'm going to clear this mess up somehow, and get you out of jail, Babe. I promise. You have to trust me."

"I trust you, but . . ."

"But what?"

"I know you're trying to make me feel better, but even you can't get me out."

CHAPTER

54

"YOU'RE UP EARLY, SIR." The Wedgewood Hotel doorman held the huge, arched glass half-door open and bowed deeply at the waist. He was young, tall, blond, handsome, and wore a tuxedo, a black top hat, and a brass name tag.

"Good morning, Carey." A sudden icy wind rippled through the leafless trees behind the government center across the street. Granz shivered, zipped up his brown leather bomber jacket, and glanced up and down Hornby.

"Can I help you find something, sir?"

"I need to be at Air Canada's offices when they open at eight o'clock."

"On West Georgia." Carey pointed. "About four blocks north, take a left, they'll be on your right, second floor. Can't miss 'em."

"Thanks."

"Looking for breakfast?"

"Just coffee."

"There's a great little coffeehouse at Hornby and Georgia. I work there weekends to help pay my UBC tuition."

"UBC?"

"University of British Columbia. Criminology student. What do you do?"

Granz contemplated lying. "I'm a cop."

"Really! Here on business?"

"Afraid so." Granz stuck his hands in his jacket pockets and turned. "Thanks for the directions."

"You bet."

Human Resource Officer Jennifer Liu checked Granz' badge and ID, then punched a few computer keys and shook her head.

"You're too late."

Granz slipped his badge case back into his pants pocket.

"What do you mean?"

"Andrea Lain's flight left Vancouver at six this morning."

"When will she be back?"

"Friday."

"Damn! Excuse me, but it's crucial that I see her today."

Liu checked the computer screen again. "She's flying to Fort St. John, Fort Nelson, turning around at Whitehorse, then back to Fort St. John at four o'clock this afternoon before starting her four off-days."

She punched more computer keys. "If it's really

important, I could book you on Flight 8593 out of Vancouver at twelve-thirty this afternoon. You could wait in Fort St. John for Andrea to get back from Whitehorse."

"That'd be great, thanks."

"We put flight crews up at the Alexander Mackenzie Inn. I'll call and make a reservation for you, then radio an in-flight message, ask her to page you when she gets to the hotel. What was your name again?"

"Sheriff Dave Granz, from Santa Rita, California." He handed Liu his VISA card. "Thanks for your help."

"No problem. Good luck, Sheriff."

Granz swung Liu's office door closed softly.

"Luck, hell," Granz muttered to himself. "We need a fuckin' miracle."

CHAPTER
55

THE DIXIE CHICKS blasted from the Alexander Mackenzie Inn's Wrangler Pub jukebox. Construction workers swigged happy-hour draft beer and watched the Edmonton Oilers trounce the New York Islanders on a big-screen TV while a crowd at the bar shot Liars Dice.

When the busboy rolled out the buffet table, Granz heaped chips, minitacos, and chicken wings on his plate and carried it to his table. He ordered a Labatt Blue, dipped a wing in ranch dressing, gnawed off the meat, and ate a second. Then the rest of them.

When the wings were gone, he inhaled the minitacos and swallowed a handful of peanuts, and dropped the shells on the hardwood floor just as the outside door opened.

A woman in an Air Canada uniform adjusted her eyes to the dark. When she spotted Granz she waved, and wove her way through the tables, stopping most of the men in midsentence.

"Hello, Sheriff." In her early forties, Andrea Lain was a gorgeous blonde in a petite but ample package; pale blue eyes, perfect skin, bright red lips, and an overbite that came off as a pout.

She motioned to the bartender, slipped off her jacket, pretending she didn't notice the eyes glued to her chest, and dropped into a chair beside Granz.

"Long day. Six takeoffs and landings. With Brit, I was usually in the air for six or eight hours at a stretch. Short hops are tough." She extended her hand.

Granz shook it. "I appreciate your coming." Her hand was soft and warm with graceful fingers and long, manicured red nails.

He finished the Labatt. The bartender handed Andrea a glass of white wine and pointed at Granz' empty. " 'Nother beer?"

"Sure."

Granz tossed a fistful of peanuts into his mouth, wishing Kathryn were there to make him savor them. "I'd like to talk to you about the incident in January. It's important."

"My Calgary flight leaves in less than two hours. Besides, I told Mr. McCaskill everything I could remember."

"I'd appreciate your repeating anything you still recall."

"Worst flight of my career. First the drunk, then the heart attack. FAA now requires us to carry defibrillaters, and the flight crews are trained to use them. If we'd had one on that flight, we might've saved him."

"You couldn't have helped, Andrea. It wasn't a heart attack."

"What do you mean?"

"Simmons died of a massive drug overdose. He was murdered."

"Murdered!" Lain stopped her wineglass halfway to her mouth.

"Didn't McCaskill tell you?"

"No, but that doesn't surprise me." She set down her glass. "What an asshole. Excuse my language."

"I've heard worse. When did he ask you to meet with him?"

"He didn't ask, he ordered."

"When was that, exactly?"

"The last weekend in January. He phoned me aboard a New York to San Francisco flight, ordered me to meet with him when we landed. Threatened to arrest me if I refused."

"You're sure about the date?"

"Absolutely. My husband and I—he's a United pilot—scheduled our days off to visit the Wine Country. The bed-and-breakfast released our reservations when we didn't show. We ended up at Knuckles Sports Bar at the SFO Hyatt. Wasn't that bad, I'm a Niners fan."

"Me, too, but you're right about McCaskill, he's a first-class jerk."

"Why don't you fire him?"

"He doesn't work for me."

"I thought you were Sheriff."

"I am, why?"

"McCaskill told me he was investigating the death for the Sheriff's Department. He had a badge, so I thought he was one of your deputies."

"He wasn't." Granz did some quick mental math, reminding himself to check on when McCaskill was appointed DA.

"Who does he work for?"

"Himself. He's District Attorney."

Andrea frowned. "Ms. Mackay told me she was District Attorney."

"She was."

"But now McCaskill is? I don't understand."

Granz stopped peeling the label off the beer bottle and set it down with shaky hands. "Kathryn's been accused of giving Simmons the drug overdose that killed him."

"Accused by whom?"

"McCaskill was appointed to replace her as DA when the evidence—all circumstantial—pointed to her. He charged her with murder. If he convicts her, she could get the death penalty."

"Did she do it?"

"What did you tell McCaskill, Andrea?"

She waited for an answer to her question, but didn't get one. "Not much he didn't already seem to know. He kept muttering to himself, even threatened again to have me arrested if my memory didn't improve. He was looking for something, but I don't know if he got it."

"I need to know exactly what you told him."

"I really have to leave or I'll miss my flight." She

glanced at her watch and stood. "He didn't tell you he taped my interview?"

"He never told anyone he interviewed you at all, much less that he recorded it. I bet the son of a bitch destroyed the tape."

She sat back down, dug in her purse, pulled out a minicassette, and slid it across the table.

"After he threatened to arrest me, I figured I'd protect myself. I had a recorder in my purse."

"Can I listen to it?"

"Take it." She stood again and put on her jacket. The construction workers stopped talking again, but she didn't notice.

Granz dropped the tape into his jacket pocket, then pulled out a folded paper and handed it to her.

"What's this?"

"A subpoena, just in case. Consider yourself served."

She dropped it into her purse. "You sure a California subpoena's valid in Canada?"

"The court in B.C. validated it," he lied.

"Sure it did."

She stood and extended her hand, and Granz shook it again, this time noting that her grip was firm and confident.

"Doesn't matter," she told him. "But, if you call me to testify, I hope you don't screw up another romantic weekend for Joe and me. And I hope my testimony shoots that jerk McCaskill in the foot."

"Me, too."

CHAPTER

56

IN HIS EARLY SIXTIES, wearing wire-rimmed glasses and tasteful slacks and a sport coat, Morgan Nelson's kindly demeanor belied his status as a nationally renowned forensic pathologist and fire-arms expert. He settled into the witness chair and waited for McCaskill's first question.

"What is your occupation?"

"I'm a forensic pathologist and toxicologist for the Santa Rita Sheriff-Coroner."

"Describe your qualifying education and training for the jury."

"I have a Master's Degree in Microbiology from Saint John's University, Doctor of Medicine from Boston University, and six years' postgraduate training in pathology and toxicology. I completed a two-

year internship at the University of Utah Hospital
and residencies in Anatomic Pathology at Boston
Hospital, Clinical Pathology at the University of
California Medical Center, and Forensic Pathology
with the Los Angeles County Medical Examiner's
Office."

"What about practical experience?"

"I was the U.S. Army Medical Corps Chief Path-
ologist at Fort Riley, Kansas, and Chief Anatomical
Pathologist at the Ninth Medical Lab at Saigon,
Vietnam. After that, Assistant County Medical
Examiner-Coroner for ten years, and Santa Rita
Sheriff's Forensic Pathologist for twenty-two years."

"Do you consult, teach, publish, or hold any special certifications?"

"I consult with the Traffic Safety Research Cor-
poration, law enforcement and forensic experts in
forty states and twenty countries. I teach at Stanford
University and the University of California, as well as
dozens of police academies. I've been published in
the *Journal of Law and Technology, Journal of Forensic
Science*, and many others. I've consulted on hundreds
of crime-scene investigations, and I'm Board-certified
in Anatomical Forensic Pathology as well as Forensic
Toxicology."

"Have you ever testified as an expert witness?"

"Almost a thousand times."

"Please explain what forensic pathology is."

"Forensic pathology is the science of interfacing
with law enforcement agencies, in assessing trau-
matic injury, and conducting autopsies."

"And toxicology?"

"Toxicology is the study of the nature, effects, and detection of poisons and the treatment of poisoning."

"Could you briefly, and as delicately as possible, explain what an autopsy involves?"

"The word 'autopsy' means 'see for yourself.' It's a surgical procedure performed by a specially trained physician on a dead body to learn the truth about the person's health during life, and how that person died. During an autopsy, every organ in the body is examined visually and, in most cases, microscopically. Blood, urine, bile, cerebrospinal and other fluid samples are taken and later analyzed. All pathological sites are photographed during the procedure."

"How long does an autopsy take?"

"Three to six hours plus twelve to fifteen hours for the microscopic and other laboratory tests."

"So, it's a very comprehensive procedure?"

"Yes."

"How many autopsies have you conducted?"

"More than nine thousand. I perform between three and five hundred per year."

"On Wednesday evening, January sixteenth of this year, did you autopsy the body of Doctor Robert Simmons?"

"I did."

"When Doctor Simmons' body was turned over to you at the Santa Rita County Morgue, were you alerted as to the most likely cause of his death?"

"Yes."

"What were you told killed him?"

"Myocardial infarction—a heart attack."

"Who told you that?"

"Kathryn Mackay."

"Tell us exactly what she said."

"That she and Sheriff Granz were bringing Simmons back from Spain to stand trial, and about an hour before the plane landed at San Francisco, he collapsed. She started chest compressions while Sheriff Granz administered CPR, but they weren't able to resuscitate him."

"When the airplane landed, the San Francisco County Coroner assumed jurisdiction, then turned the body of Doctor Simmons over to you, is that correct?"

"No, Sheriff Granz had one of his deputies drive to San Francisco and return the body directly to the Santa Rita County Morgue."

"Is that unusual?"

Nelson pursed his lips. "Somewhat."

"Did Sheriff Granz say *why*, when the San Francisco Coroner would normally have jurisdiction?"

"He said Kathryn insisted that I do the autopsy."

"Did you ask why he agreed?"

"Yes."

"What did he say?"

"He said Kathryn threatened to get a court order before they landed, if he didn't."

"Was that because you're one of her closest friends, and she thought the truth might not be discovered if you conducted the autopsy?"

Griffith objected. "Argumentative."

"Sustained," Keefe ruled.

McCaskill shrugged. "By the way, Doctor, how long have you known the defendant?"

"Twenty years, more or less."

"Professionally and personally?"

"Yes."

"She confides in you, and you do the same with her?"

"Yes."

"You consider her a good friend?"

"I certainly do."

"The defendant told you Doctor Simmons died of a heart attack, but you found no coronary heart disease, disorders, or diseases of the heart muscle or pericardium when you autopsied his body, did you?"

"No."

"What did you determine to be the cause of death?"

"Digitalis overdose."

"A massive overdose?"

"If it kills you, it's massive."

"Of course. Digitalis is a prescription heart medicine, correct?"

"That's correct."

"How is digitalis administered to a heart patient who takes it as a medicine?"

"Sometimes in pill form, sometimes by injection."

"According to your autopsy protocol, the digitalis that killed Doctor Simmons was administered orally. How did you determine that?"

"There were traces of digitalis in his stomach contents."

"What else did you find in his stomach?"

"Carbonated water, sucrose, and chemicals found in soft drinks."

"Like Coca-Cola?"

"Yes."

"Anything else?"

"No, his stomach was otherwise empty."

"So, from that information, you concluded that Doctor Simmons ingested a massive dose of digitalis along with a soft drink like Coke, right?"

"Yes.

"Doctor, would you explain to the jury what happened when Doctor Simmons was administered that massive digitalis overdose."

Nelson cleared his throat. "First, the drug dramatically increased the contraction force of his myocardium—heart muscle. Shortly after, the drug induced extreme extrastystole, or premature heart contraction, followed by uncontrolled ventricular tachycardia—excessive, rapid heartbeat—and soon after that, ventricular fibrillation—uncoordinated, arrhythmic twitching of the heart—and death."

"How quickly did death occur after Doctor Simmons was administered the digitalis overdose?"

"Almost immediately after ingestion."

"So, the person who administered the digitalis overdose to Doctor Simmons was with him immediately before he collapsed, right?"

"I'd say so," he answered softly.

"I'm sorry, I didn't hear your answer."

"Yes."

"Doctor, you're aware Sheriff Granz testified that immediately before Doctor Simmons collapsed of an apparent heart attack—which we now know wasn't a heart attack, but a fatal overdose of digitalis—the defendant was with Doctor Simmons, correct?"

"Yes."

"And that immediately after Doctor Simmons collapsed, the defendant began chest compressions and cardiopulmonary resuscitation—CPR—ostensibly in an attempt to save his life, correct?"

"Yes."

"At that point, Doctor Nelson, in your expert opinion, was there any hope of saving Doctor Simmons' life by performing those measures?"

"No."

"None at all?"

Griffith stood. "Objection, asked and answered."

"Sustained," Keefe ruled, but his eyes and the jurors' were locked on Nelson.

"Doctor, in your opinion, based on your conversations with the defendant after the remarkably similar death of District Attorney Benton, did the defendant know CPR wouldn't save Doctor Simmons' life?"

"Objection!" Griffith stood. "The witness can't testify to what my client did or didn't know."

Keefe thought for a moment. "Doctor Nelson is an expert. He can give his opinion. Answer the question, Doctor."

"She probably knew."

"So, by pretending to administer CPR on a body that she already knew was beyond help, the defendant was just putting on a grotesque show."

Before Griffith got to his feet, McCaskill smiled at the jury and said, "Strike that."

Keefe checked the clock. "Mr. McCaskill, it's almost noon. I assume you have more questions for Doctor Nelson. Is this a convenient time to break?"

"Now's fine, Your Honor."

"Very well, Court will reconvene at one-thirty." He turned to Nelson. "The witness is admonished not to discuss his testimony with anyone—including the defendant."

CHAPTER
57

Roger Griffith opened a briefcase, unfolded a linen place mat and napkin, arranged them
carefully on the table in front of Kathryn, then
unwrapped an egg salad on sourdough sandwich,
and set it on a china plate. He scooped coleslaw from
a plastic container and finally poured ice-cold milk
from a pint thermos into a crystal glass.

Kathryn raised her eyebrows. "What's this?"

"My wife and I tossed it together for you this
morning. I hope you don't mind."

"That was nice, but I'm not hungry."

"You've lost ten pounds."

"I can't eat."

"You have to. The jury can't see you fall apart."

"I feel like such a fool." She tugged at the leg of the

new navy pinstriped suit Dave and Emma had bought her.

"Sitting in court day after day dressed in damn new suits, looking brave while inside I'm so terrified I'm sick."

"Of course you're frightened, you're not Wonder Woman."

"I used to think I was, but it's not just that I'm frightened. I could handle that. I'm putting on a front while everyone I loved betrays me. It's pathetic."

"Kathryn . . ."

"Have you heard from Dave since I spoke with him in Vancouver last night?"

"No."

"Would you call him on his cell phone before court reconvenes? See if he's made any progress."

"I doubt he's contacted the stewardess yet."

"Please."

"Sure."

"Whatever she says'll probably just dig my hole deeper, anyway."

"You can't be sure of that."

"Yes I can." Kathryn started to take a bite of her sandwich, then put it down.

"Make me a promise, Roger."

"Sure."

"Once I'm convicted, start adoption proceedings for Emma and Dave immediately."

"Kate—"

"There's something else. I won't live a month on death row. You know the other inmates'll find a way to take out an ex-DA. I'd rather do it myself, but I'll need your help."

"You're asking me to help you kill yourself?"

"Call it a favor one friend does for another."

"You're talking crazy, Kate. You have to stay strong and confident."

"Strong and confident! Jesus Christ, I feel like I'm on an airplane whose engines all quit and we're plunging toward the ground at a thousand miles an hour. Disaster's imminent, but I can't bail out. If Mary Elizabeth and Dave didn't convict me, Nelson will."

"Eat your lunch." He took a bite of his burrito. "We'll get our shot at Nelson."

"That's what you said about Skinner."

CHAPTER

58

"DOCTOR, BEFORE LUNCH YOU AGREED that the defendant knew CPR wouldn't save Doctor Simmons because of conversations you had with her. In what context did those conversations occur?"

"District Attorney Benton's death."

"And Doctor Robert Simmons' alleged involvement in that death?"

"Yes."

"Did you explain to the defendant how much digitalis it takes to kill someone almost instantly?"

"Yes."

"Did you explain to the defendant *how* to administer digitalis?"

"Yes."

"So, you agree with me that the defendant knew

exactly how to administer a fatal digitalis overdose without Doctor Simmons' knowledge, and make it look like he died of a heart attack?"

"Yes but—"

"You answered the question, Doctor. The morgue is in the basement of County General Hospital, is that right?"

"Yes."

"Does the defendant ever visit you there, either for professional or personal reasons?"

"Yes."

"For both reasons, at various times?"

"Yes."

"Frequently?"

"Excuse me?"

"Does the defendant visit you at the morgue frequently?"

"Define 'frequently.' "

"On average, more often than once a year?"

"Yes."

"More than once a month?"

"Yes."

"Once a week?"

"On average, I'd say more often than that."

"Several times a week on average, then, correct?"

"I suppose so, yes."

"When the defendant visits the morgue, is she restricted to a particular area?"

"Of course not."

"Sometimes the defendant goes into your private office?"

"Yes."

"The defendant is familiar with the operation of your facility, right?"

"Yes."

"She knows where you store things?"

"Probably."

"Do you store drugs in your office at the morgue?"

"Sometimes."

"When?"

"When drugs are involved in a death, I acquire a quantity of the suspected compound for testing purposes."

"Do you lock those drugs up in a safe?"

"No."

"Why not?"

"There's no one to bother them. I don't get a lot of visitors."

"But didn't you say the defendant frequently visited the morgue, sometimes for personal purposes?"

Nelson glanced quickly at Kathryn. "Yes."

On a scrap of paper, Kathryn scribbled, "I know where he's going—I'm screwed!" and slid it over to Griffith, who read it and nodded.

"After ex-DA Benton was murdered, did you obtain a quantity of digitalis for testing?"

"Yes."

"Did the defendant know you had obtained the digitalis?"

"Yes."

"How did she know?"

"I told her."

"Was it a large quantity?"

"Yes."

"Enough to kill Doctor Simmons if someone administered it to him?"

"Yes."

"Doctor, do you still have the supply of digitalis you acquired for testing purposes after ex-DA Benton was murdered, that you told the defendant was in your office?"

For the first time, Nelson broke eye contact and looked down. "No."

"Did you dispose of it?"

"No."

"What happened to it?"

"It disappeared from my office."

"When?"

"I don't know exactly."

"No further questions."

CHAPTER
59

Judge Keefe turned to the defense table. "It's four-thirty. Maybe we should break for the day so you can cross-examine Doctor Nelson first thing tomorrow morning."

"One moment." Griffith leaned toward Kathryn. "It'll do more harm than good to cross-examine Nelson. I'm going to waive cross but reserve the right to call him as a witness when we put on our defense."

"We don't have a defense. If you let his last answer stand, the jurors will go home tonight convinced I stole the digitalis from the morgue and murdered Simmons with it. Ask him something."

"What? I just got blindsided with the stolen digitalis."

"I'm paying you to defend me. If you can't figure out what questions to ask a witness, I'll replace you with someone who can."

Griffith stared at her, then stood.

"I have only a few questions, Your Honor." He walked slowly to the podium. "Good afternoon, Doctor."

Nelson smiled, first at Kathryn, then at the jury. "Good afternoon, Mr. Griffith."

"Doctor Nelson, how many deputy coroners work for you?"

"Three."

"You contract with independent pathologists to perform autopsies when you're away on business or vacation?"

"Yes."

"Do they have keys to the morgue?"

"Yes."

"Same with the deputy coroners?"

"Yes, they have keys, too."

"How many lab technicians work for you?"

"Two." Nelson crossed his right leg over his left and leaned back in the chair.

"Do they have keys?"

"Yes. I work odd hours and am not always available when they need to get in."

"Do the pathologists, deputy coroners, and lab technicians work alone in the morgue?"

"Yes."

"On the occasions that you keep drugs in the morgue, do you lock the door to your private office?"

Nelson shook his head. "The door doesn't have a lock."

"So, you'd agree with me, Doctor, that in your absence anyone could have entered your office and removed the digitalis?"

"Yes."

"You didn't see Kathryn take the digitalis, did you, Doctor?"

"Absolutely not!"

"It could have been just about anybody?"

"Yes."

"And, as you previously testified, you don't know when it disappeared from your office, correct?"

"That's correct."

Griffith turned. "Thank you, no further questions."

Keefe looked at the prosecution table. "Redirect?"

McCaskill stood but remained at the table. "Just a couple of questions. If the pathologists or lab techs wanted to get their hands on a large amount of digitalis, they wouldn't need to rummage around in your office hoping to find some, because they have access to digitalis through their jobs, isn't that correct?"

"Yes."

"But the defendant wouldn't, right?"

"I don't know."

"Nonmedical personnel wouldn't, though, right?"

"No."

"Doctor, did the pathologists, deputy coroners, or lab techs know you had a supply of digitalis in your office?"

"No."

"But the defendant knew, right?"

"I already said I told her."

"So you did. You have no reason to believe any of the pathologists or lab techs who work for you took that digitalis, do you?"

"No."

"Given what you know today, only the defendant could have taken the digitalis, right?"

"I don't believe that."

"I admire your devotion to your friend, Doctor Nelson, but it is probable she took the digitalis, isn't it?"

"Yes."

"No further questions." McCaskill turned to Keefe. "The People rest, Your Honor."

Griffith shoved his papers into his briefcase and slammed it shut. "I should've left well enough alone!"

"I'm sorry for what I said, Roger, I didn't mean it. I'm just scared. Please don't be angry with me."

He sat beside her and put his hand on her forearm. "I'm not angry at you, Kathryn, I'm angry at myself. You aren't thinking straight—hell, under the circumstances, who can blame you. But I'm conducting the defense, and I should know better. I had no business crossing Nelson. I caved in against my better judgment, and my client—you—suffered for my bad judgment."

"Nelson killed me, didn't he? Literally."

"It's not over until the final verdict is in."

"I watched the jurors. The final verdict *is* in and it's not an acquittal, or life without parole."

"Kathryn—if you want a new lawyer, I understand. I'll move for mistrial on the basis of incompetency of counsel, buy you some time."

"I know you're not incompetent, but I don't want more time in jail, and I don't want you to move for a mistrial."

"What *do* you want me to do?"

"Grant me the favor I asked of you."

CHAPTER

60

"SIT DOWN BEFORE YOU PASS OUT."

Granz motioned to the old institutional metal chair in front of Lieutenant Aldridge's cluttered desk in the jail's office.

"Bad day."

Griffith dropped his briefcase to the floor, flung his suit coat at the rack, loosened his tie, and rolled up his shirtsleeves. "Got a fuckin' Excedrin headache, too, but no Excedrin."

Granz pulled a bottle of Tylenol PM from the center drawer and tossed it across the desk. "Looks like you need the rest."

"Thanks, Dave, I haven't slept well all week."

Griffith took four pills. "You visiting Kathryn tonight?"

"Yeah."

"When you leave, put her on suicide watch."

Granz stared. "I thought Nelson testified today."

"He did, unfortunately." Griffith massaged his eyelids hard with his fingertips.

"That bad?"

"Worse." He described Nelson's testimony. "Kathryn's convinced the jury's gonna convict."

"What do you think?"

Griffith pulled a new half-pint of Wild Turkey out of his briefcase, twisted the top to break the stamp, took a swig, and gagged. "I think she's right."

Granz frowned. "I didn't know you drank."

"I don't. Bought this on a whim, but it tastes like piss."

He screwed the top back on and handed it to Granz. "Toss it in the trash."

"Why do you think Kate needs to be watched?"

"After Nelson testified, she asked me to help her kill herself when she's convicted."

"Jesus Christ, Roger! You wouldn't do that, would you?"

"She'll spend fifteen years on death row waiting to be executed. Meanwhile, neither you nor Emma can get on with your lives. I might help if it comes to that."

"Not if I have anything to say about it."

Granz lifted the minicassette from his shirt pocket and handed it to Griffith. "Besides, maybe it doesn't have to come to that."

"What's this?"

"McCaskill interviewed the stewardess three days

before he was appointed DA. Flashed some Mickey Mouse badge, told her he was from the Sheriff's office. Didn't know she recorded it."

"You've listened to it?"

"Yeah." Granz shrugged. "No Perry Mason breakthrough, but it might open a crack you can stick your foot in."

"Wide enough to create reasonable doubt as to Kathryn's guilt?"

Granz shook his head. "Probably not."

"Enough to sway the jury against the death penalty?"

"You may be able to argue 'lingering doubt' as a circumstance in mitigation. Listen to it yourself, then decide."

"The stew's willing to testify?"

"Yeah. After I listened to the tape, I called her in Calgary. She flew back to Vancouver. She's standing by at the airport's Hilton."

Griffith dropped the tape into his briefcase, then put on his coat. "I'm headed back to my office. I'll listen to the tape on the way. If you're right that it helps, she'll be my first defense witness. Shit, she'll be my only defense witness."

"You want me to call her, have her hop the next flight to SFO?"

"Yes, just in case. What've we got to lose?"

Granz picked up the phone and started dialing. "Not a damn thing."

CHAPTER

61

"STATE YOUR NAME, please, and spell your last name for the court reporter."

"Andrea Lain, L-A-I-N."

She wore a conservative business suit, no makeup, her hair was pinned in a tight bun, and she had removed her red nail polish, but she was still beautiful. She sat erect in the witness chair, folded her hands in her lap, and made eye contact with Roger Griffith.

"What is your occupation, Ms. Lain?"

"I'm an Air Canada flight attendant."

"How long have you worked for Air Canada?"

"Two months. I flew for British Airways for almost twenty years before that."

"On January fifteenth of this year, were you working aboard British Airways Flight 287, from London Heathrow to San Francisco?"

"Yes, I was."

"What were your duties on that flight?"

"I was senior flight attendant. It was my job to tend to the passengers, oversee the other flight attendants, supervise food and drink service, and respond to incidents the other attendants might encounter during the flight."

"Did any such incident occur during that flight?"

"Yes."

"What."

"Well, first there was the drunk. I was serving drinks when a passenger got belligerent because one of the flight attendants wouldn't give him another beer. He crashed into my cart, grabbed a couple of beers, ran into the lavatory, then passed out."

"Were Sheriff Granz and Kathryn Mackay seated in your section when that happened?"

"Yes."

"Alone?"

"No. Ms. Mackay was in a window seat, Sheriff Granz was on the aisle, and their prisoner, Robert Simmons, was in the seat between them."

"How did you know Doctor Simmons' name?"

"I was alerted to his presence prior to boarding."

"How did you know Robert Simmons was a prisoner?"

"His right wrist was handcuffed to the armrest."

"You said you were serving drinks when a drunk passenger crashed into your cart, then ran into the lavatory?"

"Yes. In fact, I was serving Sheriff Granz, Ms. Mackay, and Simmons at the time. Sheriff Granz ran to the lavatory and pounded on the door, then opened it with my key. Mr. Randall was passed out, so we dragged him out and buckled him into an empty seat. Sheriff Granz checked the lavatory, and found cocaine. Mr. Randall must've been doing drugs."

Keefe leaned over the bench toward the witness stand. "Don't speculate, Ms. Lain, just stick to what you know."

"Sorry."

Griffith smiled. "No need to apologize, I do the same thing. What happened after Sheriff Granz found cocaine in the lavatory?"

"He told me to keep everyone out, then had Ms. Mackay come to the lavatory."

"When Sheriff Granz rushed to the forward lavatory, did he take Robert Simmons with him?"

"No."

"When Kathryn Mackay went to the lavatory at Sheriff Granz' request, did she take Robert Simmons with her?"

"No, she left him handcuffed to the seat."

"For how long?"

Lain thought for several seconds. "At least five minutes, maybe longer."

Griffith looked at the jury. "Ms. Lain, you're sure Ms. Mackay left Robert Simmons unattended for five minutes or more?"

"Yes."

"Thank you. When Ms. Mackay returned to her seat beside Robert Simmons, where were you?"

"I was only gone for a few minutes before I returned to the cabin to reassure my passengers that everything was under control."

"You saw Ms. Mackay return to her seat?"

"Yes, but when she returned, she sat in Sheriff Granz' seat."

"I see. When you serve drinks, do you normally hand them to the passenger in the aisle seat, and let him or her pass the drinks to the other passengers in that row?"

"Yes."

"What did Robert Simmons order to drink?"

"A Diet Coke."

Griffith leafed through several papers and frowned. "You're sure?"

"Absolutely."

"Did you see Ms. Mackay put anything in Robert Simmons' Diet Coke when she handed it to him?"

"She didn't hand it to him."

"What do you mean?"

"I had poured Simmons' Diet Coke just before Mr. Randall crashed into my cart. I set it down, but when I got back, he was drinking it."

"Who gave it to him?"

"I don't know, probably the man."

"What man?"

"When I got back, a man was standing at my cart. Said he wanted to see what the commotion was about, and he wanted something to drink."

"Did you give him something to drink?"

"He had already helped himself."

"How do you know?"

"He was holding a Coke can."

"A regular Coke or a Diet Coke?"

"Regular."

"What did the man look like?"

"Hispanic, elderly, short, a little overweight, gray hair, big mustache, bifocals."

"Could he have put something into Robert Simmons' Coke drink without your knowledge?"

"I don't know."

"But, it *is possible*?"

"I suppose."

"Did anything else happen aboard that flight?"

"I'll say. Right after Ms. Mackay returned to her seat, Simmons collapsed."

"What did you do?"

"Ms. Mackay shouted for Sheriff Granz to come, that Simmons was having a heart attack. She started chest compressions while I got an airway. Sheriff Granz administered CPR, but he was already dead."

"How long did Ms. Mackay try to revive Robert Simmons?"

"A long time, fifteen or twenty minutes, I'd guess."

"Can you describe her emotional condition?"

"Objection," McCaskill shouted. "The witness can't testify as to the defendant's emotional state."

"Your Honor, the witness has been a flight attendant for more than twenty years and is trained by the FAA to make observations and handle in-flight emergencies."

"I'll allow it," Keefe ruled.

"Ms. Lain?" Griffith prompted.

"She was highly distraught."

"What happened when it was obvious they couldn't revive him?"

"We placed his body in an empty seat for the duration of the flight."

"Did anyone stay with the body?"

"Sheriff Granz did."

"What about Ms. Mackay?"

"She returned to her seat."

"What did *she* do for the rest of the flight?"

"Cried."

"Thank you. One more question. Before Sheriff Granz spoke with you day before yesterday, in Fort St. John British Columbia, were you interviewed about the events aboard flight 287?"

"Yes."

"When?"

"Last January."

"By whom?"

"District Attorney McCaskill."

"Thank you. No further questions." Griffith turned to the bench. "The defense requests a recess."

"It's only ten-thirty. Do you have questions for this witness, Mr. McCaskill?"

"Not at this time."

Keefe stared. "Very well, court is adjourned until one-thirty this afternoon."

CHAPTER

62

"Sheriff Granz is in a briefing."

"Interrupt him."

"Well . . ." The receptionist's name tag said Lily.

"I'll take the blame, Lily."

She punched the intercom.

A tinny voice came back: "I asked you not to disturb me."

"Mr. Griffith says it's urgent, Sheriff."

Griffith leaned over the reception counter, stuck his head through the security window, and shouted loud enough to be picked up by the speaker-mike.

"Critically urgent, Dave."

He heard low voices followed by chairs sliding across the floor.

"Send him in."

When Griffith finished summarizing the flight attendant's testimony, Granz whistled. "The only helpful thing I heard on Lain's tape was that Simmons was left alone for about five minutes."

"McCaskill didn't ask the right questions, and she wasn't volunteering."

Granz leaned back in his chair. "There wasn't anything about an unknown man."

"She told me after her testimony that the guy looked weird, like maybe he was wearing a disguise."

"Why didn't she say so on the stand?"

"Said she wasn't sure, it was just a feeling, and didn't want McCaskill to go after her on it, and she wasn't sure, it was just a feeling."

"Then there's the Coke," Griffith added.

"Coke?"

"Lain poured all three of you *Diet* Cokes."

"So?"

"When she returned to her drink cart just before Simmons keeled over, the unknown man was standing there holding a *regular* Coke can."

"So?"

"Nelson's autopsy protocol report said Simmons had nothing in his stomach but carbonated water, soft-drink chemicals, and *sucrose.*"

"Sugar." Granz slid forward in his chair and leaned on his desk. "Diet Cokes use artificial sweetener, not sugar."

"Exactly."

"Randall's disturbance was staged."

"It could be coincidence, but it sounds too convenient."

"I've been a cop too long to believe in coincidence. We've got to find the man with the Coke can."

"How?"

"Jeremiah Randall's gonna tell us."

"You've got to find him first."

Granz flicked the trackball on his computer mouse to stop the screen saver and went on-line. He clicked on the California Department of Justice web site, logged in, opened the criminal records database, and called up a rap sheet.

"Randall's in custody at Soledad on a parole violation, awaiting trial on federal charges of interference with a flight crew and cocaine use."

"Won't help unless you can drive to Soledad, talk Randall into cooperating, find the Coke-Can Man, and get them back by one-thirty this afternoon."

"Stall."

"How?"

"I don't give a shit, just buy me some time."

"I guess I could move for a mistrial."

"On what grounds?"

"McCaskill concealed Lain's interview in discovery."

"Keefe'll never grant a mistrial."

"No, but he'll split the baby."

"Split it how?"

"Give me a continuance."

"For how long?"

"If I kiss his ass, a day."

"Then, french kiss it. Tomorrow's Friday, and that'd give me three days."

Griffith walked to the door of Granz' office, then

turned, hand on the doorknob. "How long does it take law enforcement to get a Department of Corrections clearance for an inmate interview at Soledad?"

Granz shook his head. "A week, more or less."

"Damn."

"I've got friends at CDC. I'll pull a few strings, try to see him tomorrow."

"Can you get in that soon?"

Granz picked up the phone. "I'd damn sure better, this may be Kathryn's last hope."

CHAPTER

63

GRANZ DROPPED EMMA AT SCHOOL, then threaded the Buick through heavy, early-Friday-morning commuter traffic. The weekend getaway to Monterey hadn't started yet, so traffic lightened up, and was moving at the speed limit, by the last Española exit.

At Moss Landing, he had to set the wipers on Intermittent to clear the thick fog from the windshield, but the sun broke through two miles later when he jogged east and merged onto U.S. 101 south.

At the outskirts of Salinas, he punched KTOM country-music radio into his stereo, set the cruise control to seventy-five, and watched the sun-bathed Gabilan Mountains roll by on the east. To the west, the craggy peaks of the Santa Lucias, still shrouded in morning fog, slipped past like apparitions.

A dozen miles later, Granz crossed the highway

and stopped at the Soledad State Penitentiary park-ing-lot entrance and presented his ID. The corrections officer in the heavily fortified kiosk inspected it care-fully, checked it against his daily visitor list, and logged Granz in with a semimilitary salute.

The prison's visitor entrance opened to a small pea-green room with a waist-high Formica counter, sev-eral file cabinets, and a couple of beat-up metal desks.

A black corrections officer named R. Robinson reinspected Granz' ID.

"Visitor list says you're here to see Jeremiah Randall."

"That's right."

He slid a clipboard across the counter. "Sign here, sir."

Granz scribbled his name above a line that read, "The Department of Corrections does not recognize hostages for purposes of bargaining with inmates."

Robinson handed Granz a temporary clip-on badge. "You been here before?"

"Yes."

"Figured. Follow me."

They passed through a heavy security gate and metal detector, then walked down a narrow hallway flanked by the prison gift shop and visitor commis-sary. At the end, a second metal door clanged open to admit the two men into an outdoor covered cage that looked, smelled, and felt like a dog run.

The second door slammed shut, then a third secu-rity door at the opposite end opened to a gravel courtyard that was surrounded by a fifteen-feet-high razor-wire fence.

"You ever interview Randall before?" Robinson asked.

Granz shook his head. "Never had the pleasure."

"Lucky you. He's a hard case, but smart. Aryan Brotherhood. Big bastard. Meaner'n my mother-in-law, too. We won't be much help if he decides to kick your ass, so I'll put you in a glass-shielded cubicle."

"Sounds good to me."

Robinson opened the door to a tiny institutional-green room and pointed at the single chair slid up close to a glass partition. There was a four-inch-diameter, mouth-high hole cut through the thick glass, and a narrow wooden ledge underneath it on both sides.

"Have a seat, they'll bring Randall in a minute. You have any trouble, or when you're finished, press that buzzer." Robinson slammed the door shut and disappeared.

A door opened on the far wall of the prisoner side of the glass. A huge white inmate glanced around, dropped into the chair on the opposite side of the glass, and sneered.

"I'm Randall."

"That's what I figured."

He was uglier than Granz remembered. He had shaved his beet-red, pockmarked face, and his head was now shaved and shined, but his gut still flopped over the top of his denim trousers. He sported a new double-lightning-bolt white-power tattoo on his forehead, and half of his left ear was missing.

Randall leaned close to the talk hole. "You're the motherfucker from the plane." His voice was high-pitched and surprisingly soft.

Granz smelled his foul breath. "I want to ask you a few questions."

"Fuck you."

"You help me, maybe I'll help you."

"Who needs your help?"

"How old are you?"

"You tell me."

"Rap sheet says forty-seven."

"Sounds about right. So what?"

"Give me a hard time, you'll never get out of the joint."

"You're scarin' me. I got less than a year left on my parole violation. The Feds'll probably drop the charges against me. Even if they don't, they ain't gonna tack much time on for no chicken-shit FAA beef or a cocaine charge."

"Maybe, but if the San Francisco DA files against you, this is your third strike. You'll go down for the rest of your life. I can work on it."

"You ain't got the juice to pull that off, man."

Granz slid his chair away and stood. "Don't bet on it."

"Wait a fuckin' minute." Randall's voice rose to a shout.

The door opened behind him. A corrections officer stuck his head in, then withdrew when Granz motioned that everything was okay.

Randall laughed. His teeth were big and yellow. "Whaddaya want to talk about?"

Granz sat down. "What went down on the plane."

"I got drunk and snorted some dope. Big deal."

"Right when Simmons gets killed? Too convenient."

"Maybe you're smarter'n you look."

"Who put you up to it?"

Randall leaned forward, elbows on the ledge in front of the glass. "I ain't givin' you what you want until I've got a deal."

Granz pushed back his chair again. "Maybe we've got nothing to talk about."

"You're bluffin' and you'd make a lousy poker player." Randall laughed. "You're fuckin' the cunt DA that's goin' down for killin' the dude on the plane and you wanna get her off, right?"

Granz' face flushed.

"Even in the joint we see the news."

"Who I fuck's none of your business."

"The hell it ain't. I can exonerate her."

Granz' heart raced. He sat down. "I'm listening."

"Here's what I want in return. First, leave my case with the Feds."

Granz shrugged.

"Second, get me transferred to Terminal Island until I'm released. Medium security and the food's better."

"I don't know how much clout I've got with the Feds."

"That's your problem, work it out."

"You forgot the cocaine."

Randall flipped his hand. "A dozen people used that lavatory before I did. Third, when my testimony springs Mackay, the Morrissey hearing that's pending against me goes away, and my parole gets reinstated."

"I'm listening, but how do I know you're not blowing smoke up my butt? You've gotta give me something now."

Randall thought. "If I give you that black judge Tucker's killer, do we have a deal?"

"I'll think about it."

"Before I was paroled, my cell mate was Eduardo Berroa. Ring a bell?"

"Maybe."

"Maybe my ass. I arranged for the little spic to escape, for a fee, of course, the day before Tucker got whacked."

"Doesn't prove he killed her."

"He bragged to me he fucked her in the ass, then cut her throat. Run the DNA from the semen in her butt against the convicted offender DNA database."

"Did that early in the investigation. There was no match."

"There's a lag time in that database. Run it again."

"What do you know about it?"

"I'm in the joint, for chrissake, not outer space. They're taking samples and submitting DNA profiles to the database every day. Inmates close to being released get done first. Berroa's parole date was comin' up. They took his blood and saliva a few days before he split. Probably hadn't caught up with the database yet."

"I'll run it again. If it matches, my deputy'll pick you up Sunday and drive you up to Santa Rita to testify on Monday."

"Deal."

"If it doesn't match, you won't hear from me again and you can rot in here."

"I'll pack tonight."

CHAPTER

64

"THIS ISN'T THE WAY TO THE—" In almost two months since her mother's arrest, Emma hadn't used the word *jail*. "To Mom's."

"I've got a special surprise," Dave teased.

"Daave! What is it?"

"If I told you, it wouldn't be a secret."

He drove slowly through town, past the Esplanade where Saturday beachgoers were loading up to head home, across the old concrete Stockton Avenue Bridge, turned onto Wharf Road, and pulled into a parking lot.

"The Shadowbrook?" Emma asked.

They climbed out and Dave locked the car doors. "I ordered takeout."

They crossed the narrow, tree-lined street. "Wanta ride the cable car?"

"Of course."

He punched the button. "Why did I know you'd say that?"

While they waited for the bright red car to struggle up from the restaurant entrance, he gazed at the beautifully landscaped grounds, Soquel Creek, the picturesque Village, and the beach beyond.

She put her arms around his waist and buried her head against his chest. "Do you think me and you and Mom'll ever come here together again?"

"A week ago, I'd've said 'no,' but now I think there's a chance."

She pulled back and looked at him. "Really?"

"I'd never lie to you."

"Something good happened, huh?"

"What makes you think so?"

"Whenever we visit Mom, you act happy, but I can tell you're just trying to make me feel good. This weekend's different."

"Different how?"

"Last night after I went to bed I heard you laughing at the TV. This morning when we took Sam for a walk, you whistled. And you called him Buddy like you used to."

"You're pretty observant for a twelve-year-old."

"I'm almost thirteen."

"Sorry."

"Is it Mom's trial?"

The cable car clacked onto the landing and disgorged three laughing couples. Dave held the door while Emma climbed aboard, then punched the Down button.

"You never asked about the trial before."

"I was scared to, you and Mom're always so grim."

"Grim's a strange word for you, Emma."

"Learned it from Mom. Last night when I talked to Mom on the phone, she sounded happy, too. Tell me what happened."

The car lurched, then started its slow descent along the Garden Path, which meandered through the manicured landscape, passed the Hillside Waterfall, stopped at the main entrance landing, then continued down the slope to intersect the footpath along the creek.

"We can't get our hopes up too much, Em. I'm not sure what it means yet."

"C'mon, Dave!"

"I'd rather let your mom talk to you about it."

The cable car screeched to a halt and the door slid open automatically. Dave grabbed Emma's elbow and escorted her to the main entry.

They stepped out of the cold onto a beige Persian rug spread out over a spacious, polished hardwood floor. The foyer was paneled entirely in native coastal redwood. The front desk was crafted from matching solid heart redwood. Dave stopped and waited.

When the young hostess appeared from the owner's private, reserved dining room in her short black silk dress, Emma punched Dave on the arm.

"I wanta be a Shadowbrook hostess."

"You and every other teenage girl in Santa Rita. Dream on."

"You and Mom know the owner, can't you put in a good word for me?"

"I would if I could think of one."

She punched his shoulder playfully.

"Good evening," the hostess greeted them. "Do you have reservations?"

"We're picking up a take-out order," Dave told her. "Granz and Mackay."

The hostess checked her list. "It'll be about fifteen minutes. If you'd like to have a drink in the Rock Room Lounge, I can take your order."

"Sure," Emma said before Dave could answer. "May I see a drink menu, please?"

The hostess looked confused, but handed Emma a stiff parchment bar menu.

"I'll have a Shirley Temple and my dad wants a Roy Rogers." Emma paused, then added, "Better make them doubles, we're celebrating."

The hostess smiled. "Celebrating what?"

"I don't know yet, he won't tell me."

"Have a seat in the lounge, I'll get your drinks."

When they found an empty table, Emma folded a napkin carefully on her lap. "Calling you Dad's easier than explaining."

Dave swallowed a lump. "Where are those drinks?"

CHAPTER

65

EMMA CLEARED LIEUTENANT ALDRIDGE'S DESK and started opening steaming containers.

"Boy, that smells good." Kathryn inspected one of the containers. "The Shadowbrook!"

"It was Dave's idea."

"What did you get us?"

Emma spread out the plates and silverware. "For appetizers, Pacific Rim prawns and Gilroy garlic fries."

"Garlic fries! People will smell you coming even if they don't see you."

Emma giggled. "Dave and Sam don't mind."

Kathryn helped herself to a prawn and a garlic fry while Emma finished setting the table. "Umm, good."

"The main course is your favorite—swordfish with pesto crust."

She uncovered another container. "I got penne with smoked chicken."

"Good choice," Kathryn observed, then picked up another container.

Kathryn ate another prawn and three more garlic fries.

"They'll smell you coming," Emma scolded.

"Touché."

"Can we talk before dinner, Mom?"

"What about?"

"Dave said something good happened, that's why him and you are so happy, but he wouldn't tell me what."

"Emma, that's terrible grammar."

"I don't care, I want to know what happened."

Kathryn thought about it. "I'm afraid of getting your hopes up, then disappointing you if it doesn't work out."

"That's what Dave said. And he said I have to be strong for you, so I don't ask about it or cry when I come to see you. But sometimes I cry when Dave and I go home, 'cause it's hard for me, too. So if there's good news, I have a right to know."

"Yes, you do. I cry, too, Em, for all of us. And you've stuck by me, so you do have a right to know. There's a man who says he knows I didn't murder Simmons."

"How does he know?"

"He says he knows who did."

"Then how come you're still in jail?"

"He has to tell Judge Keefe what he knows in court Monday."

"Then they'll let you out?"

"I don't know. The man is in prison and might be trying to get out by lying. That's why we can't get our hopes up too much."

CHAPTER

66

"No way!" Kathryn clamped her jaws, crossed her right leg over her left knee, and bounced her foot furiously, then folded her arms over her chest and gripped each biceps in the opposite hand.

"Don't be so rigid."

"What makes you think I'm being rigid?"

"Your fingers are turning white. When your mind's made up, you cross your arms and defy anyone to disagree. The last time I let you tell me how to do my job, it cost you. I won't make that mistake again."

"I'm a lawyer, too, and I think it's a bad idea."

"You aren't *your* lawyer, I am."

"If you lay out the deal Randall got in exchange for his testimony before the jury hears what he has to say, they'll never believe him."

"You'd rather I wait and let McCaskill bring it up? Have you seen Randall?"

She nodded. "On the airplane."

"He looks a lot worse now—a skinhead cross between Charles Manson and Adolph Hitler, with a swastika tattooed on his forehead for good measure."

"So?"

"If I don't bring up the deal, McCaskill will, and it'll look like we covered it up."

"I'm not suggesting you cover anything up, just wait till the jurors have had a chance to hear him out before you bring up the deal."

"How 'bout I let Keefe rehabilitate him. Judges have more clout with juries than defense attorneys."

"How're you going to do that?"

"Don't worry, I'll take care of it."

"Don't worry? Easy for you to say, it's my life on the line."

"I'm your lawyer, Kathryn, you have to trust me."

Judge Reginald Keefe surveyed the packed courtroom, ignored Kathryn Mackay, acknowledged her attorney, Roger Griffith, with a nod, greeted District Attorney Neal McCaskill, then ordered his bailiff to bring in the jury.

When they were seated, Keefe said, "Call the next witness, Mr. Griffith, if you have one."

Griffith stood. "The defense calls Jeremiah Randall."

McCaskill scanned the index to the defense investigative reports. "The defense didn't give me any discovery on Randall, nor is he on their witness list."

"I didn't know Randall was a material witness until Andrea Lain testified last Thursday, Judge,"

Griffith answered. "We located him this past week-end."

Griffith looked around and raised his voice to make sure everyone heard. "And considering McCaskill concealed Ms. Lain, the defense expects some latitude on this."

"Judge—"

Keefe held both hands out toward McCaskill to stop him, then turned toward the defense table. "No speeches, Mr. Griffith. How long will this take?"

"We won't take up too much of the Court's time."

Keefe sighed. "Very well, call your witness, but let's make this quick as possible. I want the jury to hear closing arguments this afternoon."

Granz and his deputy had removed Randall's handcuffs and leg irons in the hall, but he limped noticeably because of the two braces under his orange jail jumpsuit. He looked like he had at Soledad: big, ugly, surly, and mean. He swore to tell the truth, dropped into the witness chair, leaned back, extended his stiff legs over the edge of the stand, and crossed his ankles.

"State your name," Griffith told him.

"J.D. Randall."

"What does J.D. stand for?"

"J.D.'s what I go by."

"Indulge me."

"Jeremiah Dwight."

"Where do you live?"

"Now, or when I ain't incarcerated?"

"Now."

"California Department of Corrections."

"What is your occupation?"

"Now, or when I ain't incarcerated?"

Keefe leaned over the side of the bench and glared. "I warn you to not test my patience, Mr. Randall, because I don't have much this morning."

"I'm an electrician when I ain't incarcerated."

Randall's left upper lip curled, and he locked eyes with Keefe. "But right now I'm unemployed cuz I'm incarcerated."

"For what?" Griffith asked.

Randall waited until Keefe broke the stare-down. "Parole violation."

"For what crime had you been convicted and paroled, before you were violated?"

"Grand theft auto. Some"—he glared at Granz— "cop found a few chopped Harleys in my garage that weren't mine. I didn't know nothin' about 'em."

"Was that your first conviction?"

"Nope."

"Tell us about your prior convictions."

" 'Bout twenty years ago I got busted for an armed robbery, but I didn't know nothin' about it."

"You were convicted and spent time in prison for that, right?"

"Right."

"What else?"

"Did some time for ADW. Cops said I cut up some outlaw biker in a bar, but I didn't know nothin' about it."

"Assault with a deadly weapon?"

"Yeah."

"Why was your parole revoked?"

Randall shrugged. "Had a little trouble."

"What sort of trouble?"

"Got drunk on an airplane. They said I caused a disturbance. Some—*cop*—found blow in the head after I passed out, but I don't know nothin' 'bout that."

"By 'blow' you mean cocaine?"

"That's what the cop said, but I didn't know nothin' about it."

"You don't like police officers, do you?"

"Cops? You kiddin'?"

"I'll take that as a 'no.' Prosecutors, either, right?"

"Snakes. Worse than cops."

"How about judges?"

"Most of 'em used to be prosecutors."

"I told you to make this brief, Mr. Griffith," Keefe interrupted. "It's safe to assume a prison inmate dislikes everybody in the criminal justice system. If there's a point to this line of questioning, get to it."

"If the Court will allow me the latitude we agreed the defense is entitled to, I will, Judge."

"You'd better, and soon. Proceed."

"You're not here today because you want to help my client, District Attorney Kathryn Mackay, are you?" Griffith asked Randall.

"Not hardly."

"Why are you testifying?"

"I made a deal."

"A good deal for you?"

"I wouldn't'a made it if it wasn't."

"Did it require you to lie under oath—"

Keefe turned red. "Don't ask ridiculous questions, Counselor!"

"The defense is trying to make the point that—"

"We got the point."

"Judge—"

Keefe turned to the jury. "Ladies and gentlemen, deals are made with criminals all the time to get them to testify, but you shouldn't assume that means they necessarily lie under oath."

He returned his attention to Griffith. "Now get on with it, or I'll take over the questioning myself."

Griffith turned to look at Kathryn, who closed and opened her eyes slowly, and smiled surreptitiously.

"Yes, Judge, thank you for making my point better than I could have."

"Mr. Randall," Griffith continued, "who put together your deal?"

Randall pointed. "That cop—Granz."

"Santa Rita County Sheriff David Granz?"

"That's right."

"Did he approach you, or did you approach him?"

"He came to Soledad."

"Did he demand proof that what you're about to tell the jury is the truth, or did he just take your word for it."

"Cops never take a con's word for nothin'. He wanted me to give him somethin' before he put together a deal to prove I knew what th' f—— and that I was tellin' the truth."

"And, to get Sheriff Granz to make a deal, you 'gave him something,' to put it in your vernacular?"

"In my *what*?"

"Never mind. What did you give Sheriff Granz to convince him that what you're about to tell us is the truth?"

"The guy that snuffed Judge Tucker."

Keefe dropped his reading glasses on the bench and, reaching for them, knocked his full water glass to the floor. Ice water fell on the court reporter and ran down the front of her blouse. She jumped up and shook it off while a roar spread the room like a hurricane gathering fury.

Keefe rapped his gavel. "Silence!" He leaned over the bench. "I warned you not to test my patience. When you repeat your answer, you'll knock off the smart-ass remarks and the jailhouse jargon, and respond in language the Court and jury understand. And if you perjure yourself, I'll personally see that you spend the rest of your miserable, no-account life in prison. Do you understand that?"

Randall dropped his eyes. "Yes, sir."

"You'd better." Keefe turned to the court reporter, who was drying her transcription machine. "Read back the question."

"'What did you give Sheriff Granz to convince him that what you're about to tell us is the truth?'"

"I told Sheriff Granz who murdered Judge Tucker."

CHAPTER

67

KEEFE STOOD AND POINTED at McCaskill and Griffith.

"In my chambers. Now."

He sat behind his desk and glared at the two attorneys. "What the hell do you think you're doing, Griffith?"

Griffith handed Keefe a document.

"What's this?"

"DOJ takes blood and saliva samples from inmates convicted of violent crimes, profiles them, and stores them in the DOJ Convicted Felon DNA Database in Berkeley. DNA profiles extracted from crime scene evidence are compared to profiles in the databank."

"Tell me something I don't already know."

"Yesterday, scientists matched DNA from the

semen collected on the anal swabs during Judge Tucker's autopsy to the DNA profile of escaped inmate Eduardo Berroa. The Court may recall that Judge Tucker sentenced Berroa to state prison. I'm requesting permission to publish this report to the jury before I conclude direct examination of Randall."

Keefe loosened his tie, leaned forward with his elbows on the desk, and ran his fingers through his hair. A deep sob racked his body but Griffith and McCaskill pretended not to notice.

"That report can't come in," McCaskill protested. "It's inadmissible hearsay."

Keefe started to answer, but the words caught in his throat. He gathered himself for a moment and wiped his eyes. "He's right, Griffith. If you want it admitted, give me a relevant exception to the hearsay rule."

Griffith handed Keefe another document. "Affidavit from the custodian of records at the DNA lab in Berkeley. The report's admissible under the Business Records Exception, Judge."

"I agree." Keefe nodded. "The report goes to the jury. Now give me five minutes alone."

Griffith poked McCaskill and jerked his thumb toward the door.

Keefe slid the knot up on his tie and smoothed his hair. "Roger?"

"Sir?"

"Thank you."

"For what?"

"If you hadn't found the flight attendant, and followed the lead to Randall, I'd never know who raped and murdered Jemima."

"Just defending my client."

"I know, but still—"

"And you'd still be suspected of murdering her, polygraph or no polygraph," McCaskill interjected.

"Get out of here, McCaskill!"

CHAPTER
68

"You're still under oath, Mr. Randall," Keefe admonished.

"Okay."

"Very well." He turned to the defense table. "Proceed, Mr. Griffith."

Griffith leaned close to Kathryn, squeezed her hand, patted her on the shoulder, then walked to the podium.

"Mr. Randall, your parole was revoked because you created a disturbance on an airplane. Was that while you were a passenger aboard British Airways Flight 287, from London to San Francisco, last January fifteenth?"

"Yeah, I was hired to be on that plane."

"Hired to do what?"

"A job."

"What kind of job?"

"Stir up a ruckus while the stewardess was serving drinks, 'bout an hour before gettin' to Frisco."

"How much were you paid?"

"Twenty thousand bucks."

"Cash?"

"I don't take American Express."

Randall glanced at Keefe and grinned sheepishly. "Sorry, it slipped."

Keefe pointed his finger and frowned, but a tiny grin broke through.

"Why were you paid to create a disturbance?"

"To divert attention."

"From whom?"

"The guy they"—he pointed at Kathryn, then Granz—"had with 'em."

Griffith approached Randall and showed him a glossy eight-by-ten, black-and-white photo.

"Is this the guy?"

"That's him."

"Request this photograph of Robert Simmons be marked defense exhibit next in order."

"So ordered," Keefe ruled.

"What else were you paid to do?"

"Get them"—he pointed again—"away from the guy, Simmons, for a few minutes."

"Away from District Attorney Mackay and Sheriff Granz?"

"That's right."

"Did you know Robert Simmons?"

"No, but I seen pictures of him."

"Where?"

"Soledad."

"When?"

"Before I got paroled, and again just before that flight."

"Who showed you photos of Robert Simmons?"

"My roomie."

" 'Roomie' means your cell mate at Soledad?"

"That's what it means."

"What was his name?"

"Berroa."

"Eduardo Berroa?"

"In the slammer, we called him the Messcan Chihuahua. His real name was 'Duardo."

Griffith showed Randall a photograph of Eduardo Berroa. "Is this him?"

"Yep."

"Who paid you to divert attention and lure District Attorney Mackay and Sheriff Granz away from Robert Simmons on that flight from Spain to the United States?"

"Berroa."

"How did you know what flight Sheriff Granz, Robert Simmons, and my client would be on?"

Randall shrugged. "Berroa paid an ex-con to track Simmons down, e-mailed her with his whereabouts, then me and him went to Spain and waited. We was only two steps behind them the whole time they was in Spain. I dropped a few bucks on a ticket agent to find out what flight they was on back to the States, and we bought two tickets for the same flight."

"Did Berroa tell you why he was paying you to do this?"

McCaskill stood. "Objection, calls for hearsay."

"Overruled, it comes in as a declaration against interest. Continue, Mr. Griffith."

"He told me him and Simmons was tight once, but Simmons fucked—'scuse me, messed up his life, that it was Simmons' fault he was in the joint."

"Did Berroa tell you he planned to murder Simmons while you created a disturbance?"

"No way, man!" Randall's eyes widened and he glanced wildly at Keefe, then shook his head emphatically. "Just paid me to cause a ruckus. I didn't know nothin' 'bout no murder."

McCaskill stood again, and shook his head in disgust. "Judge, this jury can't be expected to believe Randall *isn't* an accomplice to murder."

Keefe crooked his finger at both attorneys. "Approach."

"Griffith?" he prompted.

"The accomplice rule precludes a conviction on the testimony of an accomplice unless it's corroborated by other evidence that connects a defendant with commission of the offense. Here, the killer is Berroa, not my client. The accomplice rule doesn't apply."

Keefe thought for a moment. "He's right, McCaskill. Step back."

Griffith walked close to the witness stand. "To your knowledge, did Eduardo Berroa possess a supply of digitalis?"

"Yeah."

"How do you know?"

"Berroa had me bust into the morgue. Wasn't a problem, ain't no lock on the door. Waited till it was empty one night, rode the elevator down, walked in like I owned the place, grabbed the stuff and split."

"Did Berroa tell you why he wanted the digitalis?"

"Nope. I figured he had a bad ticker."

McCaskill stood. "Objection, Your Honor. Again, we can't be expected to believe he didn't know what the digitalis was going to be used for."

"I've already ruled on this," Keefe said without hesitation. "So sit down. Proceed, Mr. Griffith."

"Mr. Randall, why should the jury believe you? You could have made all this up to get out of prison. For all we know, you murdered Robert Simmons."

"I'm a thief, not a killer."

"You knifed a man in a bar fight."

"He started it."

"How do we know Eduardo Berroa was on that flight?"

"Check the passenger list. He was next to me, in seat thirty-eight-A."

"Under his own name?"

"No, Fernando Villanuevo. Check it out."

"I did." Griffith handed a paper to Keefe and a copy to McCaskill.

"A certified passenger manifest for January fifteenth British Airways Flight 287," he explained. "It shows the passenger in seat thirty-eight-A was Fernando Villanuevo. Request this document be marked defense exhibit next in order."

"So ordered. Continue, Mr. Griffith."

"What else can you tell the jury that will prove to

them that what you say today is the truth, Mr. Randall?"

"Eduardo Berroa murdered Judge Tucker."

A loud, collective roar arose in the courtroom, which Keefe silenced with his gavel, then he directed Griffith to go on.

"Do you know when?"

"The day after Berroa 'scaped from Soledad. Early in January. Friday night."

"Could it have been Friday, January eleventh?"

"Sounds right."

"Do you know *where* Berroa murdered Judge Tucker?"

"In her chambers, here in this building."

"Did Berroa tell you *how* he murdered her?"

"Slit her throat with a scalpel he stole from the prison infirmary before he 'scaped."

Keefe squeezed his eyes shut and rubbed them with his fists.

Griffith waited for Keefe to recover, then continued. "Did Berroa tell you whether or not he raped Judge Tucker before he killed her?"

"He raped her all right, prison style."

"By 'prison style' you mean he raped her anally?"

"Right. The little spic—'scuse me, Judge, Berroa was a whore—lots a'guys had him in the slammer. Wanted her to know what it felt like."

Griffith picked up the DNA report. "At this time, Your Honor, I wish to publish this report to the jury."

When he finished, he turned back to Randall. "One final question. Did Eduardo Berroa tell you *why* he murdered Judge Tucker?"

McCaskill started to object, but Keefe silenced him with a glare.

"To get even with her for sending him to prison."

"No further questions, Your Honor," Griffith said. "At this time the defense requests that the Court order the entry of a judgment of acquittal of murder because the evidence is insufficient to sustain a conviction on appeal."

Keefe rotated his chair toward the prosecution. "Mr. McCaskill, I'll hear argument now."

"If you believe Mr. Randall, that Eduardo Berroa, not the defendant, murdered Doctor Simmons, then it is unreasonable to believe that Mr. Randall is himself not liable for prosecution of Doctor Simmons as an accomplice to murder."

McCaskill glanced at Mackay and as quickly turned away. "An acquittal pursuant to Penal Code Section 1118.1 cannot be granted based on the testimony of an accomplice unless his testimony is corroborated by such other evidence as tends to connect Eduardo Berroa to the murder of Doctor Simmons."

"Mr. Griffith, I'm afraid McCaskill is right. Let's recess till tomorrow to see if you can find us some corroboration."

CHAPTER

69

"THE DEFENSE RECALLS ANDREA LAIN."

She wore expensive tan slacks, a beige silk blouse, and no makeup, and her long blond hair hung loosely around her shoulders. She wasn't smiling.

Griffith had her sworn, then apologized for interrupting another trip to Napa with her husband by subpoenaing her the night before.

"Ms. Lain, you previously testified that on January fifteenth of this year, you were senior flight attendant on British Airways Flight 287. Would you recognize the passenger who created a disturbance aboard that flight?"

"Yes."

"Permission to approach the witness?"

When Keefe nodded his assent, Griffith handed Lain a photograph. "Is this the man?"

"It is."

"Do you recall the man's name according to the passenger manifest?"

"Jeremiah Randall."

"Would you also recognize the passenger who sat beside Mr. Randall on that flight?"

"Yes."

Griffith handed her a picture of Eduardo Berroa. "Is that him?"

"Yes."

"In your previous testimony you said he was older, with gray hair and mustache."

"He was disguised. This is him."

"You're certain?"

"Absolutely. I returned to the cabin after the disturbance to assure my passengers that everything was under control. He asked how Mr. Randall was doing."

"Why didn't you mention this when you testified the first time?"

"I didn't remember until now."

"Did you see Eduardo Berroa earlier during that flight?"

"Yes. I saw him standing beside my drink cart holding a Coke can, immediately before Robert Simmons collapsed."

The room was silent.

"No further questions."

"Questions, Mr. McCaskill?" Keefe asked. "Or may this witness be excused?"

"Excuse her."

Griffith waited until Lain had left. "The defense

renews its motion that the Court order a judgment of acquittal of murder in favor of my client, on the basis that the evidence is insufficient to sustain a conviction on appeal."

Keefe rotated his chair toward the prosecution. "I don't need to hear from you, Mr. McCaskill."

He turned to the defense table. "The Court declares the evidence against the defendant, Kathryn Mackay, insufficient to sustain a conviction thereon, and orders a judgment of acquittal be entered.

"This Court further orders that Kathryn Mackay be reinstated from administrative leave immediately and returned to the position of Santa Rita County District Attorney."

The courtroom erupted in a sea of flashbulbs and camera lights.

Griffith stuffed papers into his briefcase and snapped it shut. "The media's going to demand interviews."

"I'll meet you in a minute," she told him.

"Your Honor?"

Keefe sat back down at the bench. "Ms. Mackay?"

"I request that Mr. McCaskill be taken into custody for violation of Penal Code Section 128, procuring the prosecution and execution of an innocent person."

McCaskill glanced around the room like a rat trapped in a maze, looking for a way out.

"Bailiff, arrest Mr. McCaskill," Keefe ordered.

"You can't—" McCaskill started to protest.

Keefe cut him off. "I'll need a complaint filed by five o'clock this afternoon, Ms. Mackay."

"You'll have it."

CHAPTER
70

"FIGURED YOU WOULDN'T BE GOING TO LUNCH."
Dave set a fresh cup of Starbucks coffee on Kathryn's
desk.

"You heard Keefe. I file my complaint against
McCaskill by five P.M. or he'll be released."

Dave flipped his hand dismissively. "McCaskill's
not going anyplace. You should take some time off,
put all this behind you."

"The only way to do that is by getting my life back
to normal, and that means working."

Dave sipped his coffee. "You gonna indict Berroa
for Simmons' murder?"

"Damn right. Tucker's, too. I'll convene the Grand
Jury this week. I'm going to convict him of two murders
as soon as you catch up with him and bring him back."

"Me? I would've bet you'd do it yourself."

"I learned my lesson the hard way." She paused. "From now on, you do the police work and I'll do the prosecuting."

"Deal. Will you ask for the death penalty?"

"No."

"Berroa killed Simmons by poisoning."

"I know, and I can admit it now—I agree with McCaskill that administration of a lethal dose of digitalis meets the legal requirement."

"Berroa murdered Tucker and Simmons. Multiple murders is also a special circumstance. If anyone deserves the death penalty, he does."

"I'd have agreed a few months ago. Not anymore."

"California law calls for the death penalty for certain crimes. As DA, you can't ignore that."

"When it comes to what charges are filed, California law vests considerable discretion in the DA. I'm not required to ask for a death sentence. The death penalty's inhumane—barbaric. For me, it was always about an 'eye for an eye.' I'll never see it that way again."

He stood and dropped the coffee cup into the wastebasket. "I oughta get to work myself."

Before he reached the door, she stopped him. "Let's go out to dinner tonight, Babe."

"Sure, where?"

"The Shadowbrook."

CHAPTER

71

THE CABLE CAR SCREECHED to a stop at the Shadowbrook's main entrance. When the door slid open, a man was waiting on the landing.

"Good evening, Dave. Kathryn. Emma. I have your table ready."

"Thanks, Ted, but we didn't make reservations."

"It's taken care of. This way, please."

The hostess smiled as they passed. "Hi, Emma."

"Hi."

"You know her?" Kathryn asked.

"She waited on us when we picked up the take-out."

Ted escorted them to a window table overlooking the Creek and Village. Through the evening fog, the sun painted the horizon with bold, brilliant, overlapping strokes of orange, yellow, and red. A bouquet sat in the center of the linen-covered table beside a bottle of Bargetto champagne in a frosty china cooler. With the evening light in the background, tiny bubbles leaped from the neck of the bottle like frightened fireflies.

"Your usual, Emma?" Ted asked.

"That'll be fine."

"A Shirley Temple it is. I assume your parents prefer the champagne."

Kathryn read the card from the bouquet. " 'Best wishes, Roger.' How did he know we were coming here?"

"He called this afternoon and invited us to join him and his wife. I told him some other time."

The hostess brought Emma's Shirley Temple and filled two fluted, stemmed glasses with champagne. Dave lifted his glass and touched it first to Emma's, then to Kathryn's.

"To you."

"To our family," Kathryn corrected.

They sipped their drinks for several minutes. When the waiter came, Kathryn told him she hadn't decided.

"She always orders last," Emma explained. "I'll have steak Diane, medium."

"Very good. You, sir?"

"Prime rib. Rare."

"What about you, ma'am?"

"Pacific Rim prawns for an appetizer and pesto-crusted swordfish."

"Excellent choice."

"Mom, you're in a rut, that's what you had Saturday night."

After dinner, they stood on the landing waiting for the cable car, shivering in the cool spring-night air.

"I need to go back inside," Emma told them. "I'll meet you at the car."

"For what?" Kathryn asked.

"To ask the hostess how to get a job like hers, and where to buy the dress."

"You're too young to get a job," Kathryn told her.

"What do you think, Dave?" Emma asked.

"Shoulda got a job years ago, you slacker."

Dave started the car's engine and flipped on the heater. "Should we start looking for a new home, Babe?"

"Do we have to decide tonight?"

"Nope. When?"

"Next time we're lying on some tropical beach sipping piña coladas."

CHAPTER

72

"Is it always this hot?"

"No, Señor."

"When does it cool down?"

"At night."

"I'd better have another one of these." Dave held out his glass.

"Bueno, una mas piña colada. ¿Y tú, Señora?

"I'll stick with another frosty-cold bottled water," Kathryn told him.

"¿Que?"

"Agua fría, por favor."

"Sí, Señora."

"You look great in your new bikini, Babe, but there's one problem."

She shaded her eyes against the intense sun that,

as it dropped toward the horizon, bounced off the mirror-glass-smooth surface of Tangolunda Bay.

"What problem?"

"This place isn't topless."

"Our room is."

"What about our drinks?"

"Would you rather have another piña colada or me?"

"I wasn't thirsty anyway." He held out his hand and helped her out of her lounge chair, then as he straightened up he smashed his head on the underside of the palapa.

"Ouch! Palm fronds aren't as soft as they look."

They walked hand in hand up the winding, flower-lined path of the Camino Real Zaashila Resort Hotel. Dave stopped at the foot of the stairs that led to their third-floor villa, and held a bunch of delicate, fragrant white flowers to his nose.

"These things grow everywhere, and are the most beautiful things I've ever smelled. What are they?"

She tugged at his arm. "Aphrodisiacs."

Afterward, they lay on the bed silently, then showered together and made love again under the cool water.

Dave pulled on fresh white shorts and T-shirt. "Where should we eat?"

"Let's take a taxi to La Crucecita, stroll through el zócalo, then eat at our favorite restaurant."

"Which favorite—María Sabina or Los Portales?"

"You decide. Then let's pick up something at the bakery for tomorrow's breakfast before we head back to the resort."

"Emma's right about you getting into ruts, Kate. We've done that every day for a week, aren't you tired of it?"

"No. We've made love every day for a week, but I'm not tired of that, either. I'd like to stop at the church before we head back to the resort."

"We've already looked at the Virgin of Guadalupe painting on the ceiling of the church."

"This time I want to pray. To give thanks."

"For what?"

"Being so lucky. Freedom; Emma; you. Our new family."

"You said next time we were lying on a tropical beach drinking piña coladas, we should talk about buying a place of our own. Wanta discuss it now?"

"Let's go back to our room, sit on the veranda, look at the ocean and enjoy our last night in Huatulco."

After Kathryn prayed, they stopped at a plaza shop and bought Emma a hand-painted doll.

Dave slid his arm around her waist. "After we sit on the veranda awhile, do you want to make love?"

"Yes."

EPILOGUE

"I TRUST YOU ENJOYED YOUR STAY at Camino Real Zaashila?"

They looked tanned, rested, and happy.

Dave nodded and handed his VISA card to the clerk. "Very much."

The clerk processed the credit card and handed it back. "I'll arrange transportation to the airport."

"Gracias."

"De nada. Please visit us again soon."

"We will, señor." Kathryn picked up her handbag, and led Dave to the taxi stand outside the huge palapa lobby.

He tossed the wrinkled Polaroid photo of Emma Mackay in the trash, straightened the bifocals, pushed his floppy *hat down over the gray wig, and smoothed the false gray mustache.*

"Don't make promises you can't keep," he muttered. "I got Tucker and Simmons. You're both next."

The clerk glanced at him. "Excuse me, señor?"

"Nada. Estaba hablando solo."